You'll Catch Your Death

You'll Catch Your Death

NEW STORIES BY HUGH HOOD

The Porcupine's Quill, Inc.

CANADIAN CATALOGUING IN PUBLICATION DATA

Hood, Hugh, 1928-
    You'll catch your death

ISBN 0-88984-144-6

I. Title.

PS8515.O64Y68 1992   C813'.54   C92-094216-4
PR9199.3.H66Y68 1992

Published by The Porcupine's Quill, Inc., 68 Main Street, Erin,
Ontario NOB 1TO with financial assistance from The Canada
Council and the Ontario Arts Council. The support of the Government of Ontario through the Ministry of Culture and Communications is also gratefully acknowledged.

Distributed by General Publishing Co. Ltd, 30 Lesmill Road,
Don Mills, Ontario M3B 2T6.

Readied for the press by John Metcalf.
Copy edited by Doris Cowan.

Cover is after an untitled pastel drawing by Noreen Mallory, 1991.

Typeset in Ehrhardt, printed and bound by The Porcupine's Quill.
The stock is acid-free Zephyr Antique laid.

For my teacher,
Noreen Mallory

Contents

More Birds

I HAD GONE DOWN from Bologna to Ravenna for the day, intending to look for cheap lodgings near the station which I might reserve for a more extended visit later in the month. It was my first approach to the shores of the Adriatic and I remember with pleasure how the country flattened out after we left Bologna, the shadowy Apennines eventually disappearing away off to the right. The train, a slow local which left the main line at Castel Bolognese, wound its way over the flat land and across a series of minor rivercourses, under the warm golden sunlight of a perfect May afternoon. One of the rivers we crossed was the Rubicon. There was a small finger-sign bearing the name of the historic site set at a crazy angle in the cement base of the railway bridge. It had been a protracted, extremely dry spring, and there was almost no water in the famous riverbed; anybody might have crossed it at any time.

The countryside round about and the little towns on the branch railway are heavenly places. Faenza, where faience originated, Forli, Savignano on the banks of the Rubicon, set down on those sunny grassy flatlands nearer and nearer to the coastline and the Adriatic capitals, Ravenna, Rimini. After a while I began to have a strong sense of the proximity of water. I could smell the marshlands and now and then catch the cry of some wandering waterbirds. We ran into Ravenna station with a rush, and I was surprised to see three or four coasting steamers moored in a turning basin on the other side of the railway line. I hadn't realized that seagoing vessels could make their way right up the channel to the old town.

I came out of the station, crossed the piazza and strolled along the Via Farini, a wide splendid boulevard, towards the Via Rocca Brancaleone where, my experience suggested, the nearest hotel district might be found. I saw a sign not far off which said 'Jolly Hotel' in large elegant letters. I wouldn't stay in one of the hotels of the expensive Jolly organization but I'd be sure to find a more modest establishment close by, as indeed I did, the Albergo Giaciglia, open barely a month, gleaming with fresh varnish and new plumbing, a family operation in the hands of an engaging young proprietor and his even younger wife, who did all the chambermaiding. I closed with them immediately on the terms of a reservation for an extended stay through the end of May, telling them that I would go back to Bologna that evening to collect my belongings, and would be back in Ravenna in a day or two.

Satisfactory arrangements were sealed by a small down payment against my reservation, roughly the cost of a single night's lodging. The proprietor and his wife, between them interpreting my shaky Italian, now directed me in the direction of S. Vitale. I had two hours at my disposal this afternoon, they said. Why not pass the time in examining one or two of the celebrated sights of the old imperial capital? The Arian Baptistery perhaps? S. Vitale and the mausoleum of Galla Placidia were also well within walking distance and would amply reward a two-hour visit. They came out into the Via Brancaleone with me, grabbed my elbows, guided me to the end of the block and pointed me along the Via Paolo Costa in the direction of the site. We parted with many expressions of mutual good will. I found that I had a very brief walk to accomplish. Ten minutes of easy sauntering, following a series of unambiguous signs, brought me to the grounds of S. Vitale. Without paying very much attention to where I was going, I passed through the narrow and unpretentious gates, crossed a modest lawn of thick, almost rank grass, and entered the building, at that moment vividly lit up by a sequence of those automatic lighting devices employed to extract coins from the touristical purse. You deposit a stipulated sum in the slot and the superb mosaic lights up above you like the vision of a judgement duly paid for.

I was thunderstruck. No woman or man alive can draw the interior of S. Vitale. The thing is impossible; the interior can't be taken in from a single viewpoint. Never mind the inexhaustible splendour of the mosaic. The bewildering sequences of curves and angles, pillar and arch and aperture and ambulatory, comprise the subtlest interior design I have ever seen. My head swam. At intervals a coin would click into a box and lights would come on here or there. I saw saints and I saw birds, if anything more birds than saints, and these birds appeared to move in appalling animation although naturally they weren't moving at all. To give myself some respite from the swirling dizzying attractions of the forms in the air around me, I turned into a shadowy corner and followed a trail of visitors into the postcard and souvenir shop. I intended to make a small collection of coloured cards of the interior of the building which I might then paste on the kitchen wall of my apartment at home. My eyes tracked up and down the ranked racks of postcards; what I saw was mosaic renderings of birds and birds and again birds. I collected thirty-three pictures of birds, all different, in three minutes. Birds or other kinds of winged creatures cast in the forms of birds.

First of all I spotted the four Evangelists, pictured with their wings extended and half upright, as though they were aquatic birds swimming in a midnight firmament lit by a myriad of golden lights winking in a paradisal blue: at the centre of the vaulting heaven the golden cross of the dome of Galla Placidia. The figure of Saint Mark floats on the lower right side of the central cross with feathered wings poised for takeoff, head and torso of a golden lion, clouds rippling beneath the swelling breast as though he swam on water – passages alternately of striped red and white cloudlets or waves. Stony hints of brilliant red gleam in the lion's eyes and mouth, but the body and wings are those of a gentle golden dove.

The forms of the other Evangelists seem rather to emerge on the surface of the firmament, as though after submersion, than to float on it like the winged lion. Saint John is figured with an eagle's head, a single visible eye carried out in flecks of red, white and blue stone, the expression of the eye profoundly birdlike, very much that of certain parrots I have known, interrogative and searching.

The mausoleum of Galla Placidia, about fifty yards away across the little garden from S. Vitale, is filled with the forms of birds. Two famous pigeons perch with unaffected casualness on the edge of a white stone ewer or birdbath, its edge rimmed with brightly decorative red, the waters within pictured in exquisite blue and red. What are those pigeons doing there, so evidently unbidden guests, at the same time essential participants in the great scene of martyr and confessor contemplating the eternal stars? Why pigeons, why drinking? The same pigeons, filled with the animation of everyday existence, swarm in the streets of Ravenna as they did 1500 years ago when the mausoleum was built to house the long sleep of an emperor's mother.

Though there were pigeons abundantly in circulation on the streets of the little city when it was the imperial capital about the year 450, there may not have been peacocks roaming loose, nor herons, pelicans or parrots. These have found their way into S. Vitale from some imaginary aviary of the artistic consciousness, swarming and dazzling in their colour and variety. Now the birds of Ravenna carol in my dreams.

They fill the air with their glorious many colours and their songs. They are somehow or other God's joke with us (not *on* us), the birds. Jokes are the signs of pure being; we expect things to be as they are – whoever could have predicted the birds – and laugh with surprised delight when they are not. There needn't have been any birds at all. The Almighty thought of them and in that moment brings them to existence, which He needn't have done. Perhaps they are the supreme expression of loving freedom. Imagine a world without them! In the mosaics of Ravenna and Classe they are everywhere, cranes conversing amiably with turtles, peacocks with fanned-out blue stone tails spread like sprays of jewels on high curved cupolas. Doves and pigeons and parakeets and pelicans and peacocks, and they all mean something, I expect.

I found them exhilarating to contemplate and I made a mental note to drop back into the office of the Albergo Giaciglia and extend my reservation. I saw at once that I couldn't do Ravenna, those mighty tombs, in the inside of a week. I made a few hasty and ineffective pencil sketches of the mausoleum and the basilica, laughing at the contrast between the inconspicuous red brick exteriors and the extraordinary displays within. The brick increased greatly in magnificence as one's consciousness of what it concealed grew more and more intense. The interiors are impossible to render in a sketch, and you might think it easier to do the outsides, but you would be wrong. The two small unassuming structures are miracles of line; you can't judge them with perfect accuracy because the level of the ground around them is several feet higher than it was when they were built. This modification of their position has altered the relationships of their lines, giving them a weirdly handsome disproportion.

Some time later I compared my sketches to a group of colour photographs in a travel brochure. In my impatience to get the form of the mausoleum on paper, realizing that there wasn't time to sketch in the texture of the brickwork, I had left most of the walls white, simply indicating the lie of the brick in a few places, as one might attach a swatch of material to a costume sketch. I was left with a Galla Placidia which rejoiced in walls of gleaming white, with borders of brick-red. This rendering, quite false to the actual state of the building, was strangely suggestive of the look of the place fifteen hundred years ago, when the foundation walls hadn't been silted up and the sky inside was new in its blue glory.

I am at best an amateur sketcher; there could be no question of producing an accurate representation of either structure. All the same, my sketches coincided to a remarkable degree with the look of the buildings as photographed. I think that the formal perfection embodied there will thrust itself upon any eye, mechanical or living. For once the perceptions of the camera and of human sight will coincide, as happens very rarely, always in the contemplation of some great radiance of form. The lovely face of Mia Farrow or Lillian Gish will appear lovely to the eye, the camera, to saint and sinner alike.

At the Albergo Giaciglia they made no difficulties about assigning me space for a few extra days. Tourism had suffered that summer on account of nuclear disaster in the Ukraine, terrorist hijackings in Milano and elsewhere. Hotel space was by no means at a premium, as the proprietor explained. He sat me down – almost forcibly – in his little dining room, fetched me a cappuccino, *molto caldo,* and launched into a dissertation on the sickly state of the tourist trade. I sipped one cup, then a second, and began to wonder about train times. Once or twice I might have glanced at my watch as unobtrusively as I could, but Armando Bortoletto drew out his account of his professional difficulties with easy persuasiveness, and I couldn't choose but hear. He was in full control of the situation, and at length urged me to my feet – refusing all offers of payment for my two cups of coffee – and once more accompanied me along the street as far as the Via Farini. He indicated the railway station with an expansive gesture and started me on my way with a gentle push. We might have been old schoolfellows or natives of the same marshland village, so intimately friendly was his smile, his readiness to assist.

This fine Italian subtlety! He had kept me in conversation for precisely the right length of time, about forty-five minutes, so that I arrived in the station with just five minutes to spare before the local train departed at 4:16. This time I couldn't go directly to Bologna; there would be a change and a thirty-five-minute wait at Castel Bolognese for the through train coming from the south. I didn't mind. I had no evening appointment barring a vague inclination to dine at Pippo's, where the Bolognese cuisine gave daily of its finest. I thought of the series of delightful meals I had enjoyed in Bologna, and for a moment my bad old Canadian conscience spoke uneasily to my senses. I was enjoying myself just slightly too much. No good could come of that.

At 4:14 the local train ambled into the station, its blue paint shining smoothly in the afternoon sun. One of the coasting steamers lying in the basin across the tracks was painted the identical shade of blue; both recalled the marine heavens of Galla Placidia. Impressions coalesced smoothly in my imagination. I climbed into the almost empty train and we moved off strictly according to schedule. In my experience, Italian trains keep to their announced times of arrival and departure. We were due in Castel Bolognese at five, and we arrived on the hour. We were now some miles further inland than at Ravenna; the late afternoon sun seemed suddenly drier and much warmer. The rays of the declining sun were almost palpable, long bars of gold stretching across the fields, reflected brilliantly from terra-cotta roofs and brightly coloured stucco. The station platform might have been dusted in its stillness with a fine golden powder. I strolled up and down the platform with half an hour to kill; there seemed nobody around. I sank down on one of the empty benches towards the southern end of the platform. If it hadn't been for those two cups of cappuccino I'd have fallen asleep. I might still be sitting there.

The minute hand of the platform clock made a faint click every sixty seconds as it jumped forward to a new position. I could hear this from quite a distance as I drowsed with my eyes half shut, until after ten or a dozen clicks I started to be conscious of another, less familiar sound which, slowly at first and then with increasing intensity, took the form of a peculiar treble outcry, many-voiced and eerily unfamiliar. The sound made its steady way into my head; at first I dismissed it, then I wondered what it might be, then I made a tentative identification. Puppies, somebody's pets, perhaps bothered by ticks or fleas.

But it wasn't quite the sound of puppies; it was something else. It was getting on towards train time anyway, so I got slowly to my feet and looked around me for the source of the noise, small cries, pipings. I strolled comfortably along the platform past the entry-way and the stationmaster's office and the *tavola calda*, keeping my ears pricked up for the sound of some deeply alarmed living crea-ture, and then I realized where these were coming from.

Up at the north end of the platform stood a row of those iron-wheeled freight wagons which are used on railways everywhere to shift small bulk shipments from trucks to railway cars, and vice versa. They have a long-tongued handle, four heavy wheels, and slightly slanted metal rims at the edges of the wagon bed to tilt the load inwards. Three wagons were parked one after another at a point which would allow for prompt loading onto the northbound train which was due shortly. At first I didn't quite grasp the nature of the wagonload. It seemed to be a collection of flat cartons piled on top of one another, six or seven cartons high, with two piles to each wagon.

The cartons were about five feet by four and six to seven inches in height; they were made of heavy waxed cardboard with metal binding at the corners, and a sequence of airholes, each about the size of a silver dollar, punched along the sides. I guess there were twelve cartons on each wagon, over thirty in the whole consignment. I put my hand on the surface of the nearest one, at the bottom of a pile. It was warm, even hot, to the touch. I hadn't noticed the wagons when I came onto the platform. Maybe they'd just been wheeled into place a few minutes ago from some nearby warehouse or staging platform. I still hadn't identified the sounds coming from inside the boxes. It couldn't be puppies; there wasn't enough height to the boxes to allow puppies to stand or sit in them. Nobody ships thirty cartons of puppies without water or feed.

The outcry from the boxes grew shriller, more varied, more alarmed, as I approached. Whatever was inside seemed to know that I was there. The cries began to diversify themselves, some lower and others higher in pitch. I sensed a peculiar orchestration in their phrasing, as though the creatures were calling out to one another. I stepped up beside the first wagon and, shading my left eye with a hand to my forehead, I squinted into one of the airholes. At first the transition from bright sunlight to shadow made it impossible for me to focus on what was inside, but then my eye adjusted to the darkness of the interior of the boxes and I saw what I'd come to expect, a tiny glaring red-rimmed eye, intensely expressive, terrified, peering through the hole at me. There was a series of sharp scuffling noises, the flutter of wings.

Thirty cartons of birds pressed down, sandwiched together, trapped in the heat and the dark, all tumbled together in heaps, some with damaged wings, some dying of thirst, all terrified and unable to imagine where they were or what was happening to them. I couldn't find a place where two airholes were close enough together for me to look in with both eyes. I may have gotten a somewhat partial view of the situation because I had only one eye available but I don't think so. I glimpsed many different species of birds. I saw lovebirds, but not in their natural pairs. If they had formed their bond before shipment, that bond would certainly be obliterated under these conditions. No bird, no matter how attached to a mate, would be able to remain beside it in such a situation.

I'm sure there were parakeets because I could hear sharply-pitched, very human phrases calling out of the darkness. I tried to find the feeding arrangements – trays of seed, troughs for drinking – but I couldn't locate any. I suspected that the birds were being shipped on a survival-of-the-fittest basis. If six hundred birds were crammed into the shipment, as many as three hundred might survive the trip, enough for the shipper to realize a handsome profit at commercial rates. The three hundred dead could simply be swept out of the cartons and disposed of. If no food, water or means of keeping clean were provided, shipping costs would be minimal. The cartons were probably heavy enough to be reusable. I stepped back from my improvised spyhole and walked along the row of wagons. It was clear that they had been used before; they were certainly made specially for this traffic. They had been numbered according to some sort of shipping code in black felt pen. Addresses in Bologna were visible here and there on stapled labels. At least the birds hadn't much further to go.

I peeked in at several other airholes. I'm certain that I saw doves. I saw pigeons. Why anybody would try to market pigeons commercially in Italy is beyond me; you might pick one up off the street for free just about anywhere. Carrying pigeons to Bologna would be about like carrying coals to Newcastle, except that nobody ships anything to Newcastle any more. It's a dying city.

In a few of the boxes bigger birds were imprisoned. I believe that I identified certain parrots that measure as much as twenty inches overall. Think of confining such a creature in such a space! They were terrified. Sometimes they all seemed to cry in unison. Then the smaller birds would subside and there would be screeches from the big parrots. Then a wave of outcry would pass along the row of wagons, seeming to pour out of each airhole. This would merge into a chaotic unmusical yapping, the sound that had made me think of whipped puppies, from hundreds of straining throats.

I began to think of the trains to the camps. I thought of the darkness inside the cars, the smell of the bodies bumping together in the dark. The unknown destination. The obscure fate. An occasional gleam of light through a splintered wall panel, the terrified eye pressed against the gap, red-rimmed, inflamed.

We will do anything, you know. Absolutely anything.

I know something about birds. I've lived with them and loved them all my life. I thought, perhaps I can calm them, and I started to whistle to them in sequences of musical notes that I've learned over many years of observation. Maybe they would be soothed and charmed by the music. I set my lips and trilled and produced the sweetest tones that I could manage. It was like a miracle. All along the row of wagons the frightened cheepings and screechings began to slow down and then to disappear. I found myself whistling bird-calls heard more often on the banks of eastern Ontario rivers than in Castel Bolognese, and the outcry softened and died away and I felt a great triumph in my heart. I whistled for dear life.

But the train for the north was due and on time, and I had to leave. I hoped that the birds would be coming along in the baggage car of my train. Their journey would be over in another hour. Then they would be fed and watered, cleaned and exercised, at least I hoped they would. The train from Rimini drew into the station and I had to stop whistling and turn away as a pair of railway attendants appeared and began to pull the big wagons across the platform towards the stationary baggage car.

I walked along the platform towards the first-class carriages in the middle of the train; they seemed nowhere near half full. I turned to mount the stairs into a carriage and out of the corner of my eye I saw the three big wagons parked beside an open loading port. I could hear the birds' agonized outcries starting up again and I thought of trying to get into the baggage car so that I could go on whistling to the poor things all the way to Bologna, but I took the turn into the first-class car almost without hesitation. They'd think I was out of my mind if I turned up in the baggage car with a request like that. The birds wouldn't be able to hear me anyway, not over the sound of the train in motion. I might as well give it up.

I wondered if anybody would give them food and water on this leg of the trip. There was only an hour to go, but it suddenly struck me that it was now past normal business hours. I doubted that any-body would come to the station to collect the shipment this late in the day. They would just be left in a shed overnight, perhaps much longer.

I tried to put these thoughts out of my mind, turning my attention to the beauties, almost the luxuries, of the car in which I was riding. The windows were finely shaped, the whole of the interior of the first-class carriage something of a triumph of contemporary Italian design. Carried out in deep mellow tones of blue and red, with seats elegantly upholstered in a firm black pile, practically brand-new and spotlessly clean, the carriage was designated as a non-smoking vehicle. There was probably a smoking car right behind us. The train from Rimini wasn't one of the TEE trains, nothing so spectacular as that, but it moved very smoothly at a rapid pace and the interior of the carriage was everything a traveller might wish for, airy, fresh-smelling, quiet, not very full of passengers. There were only a few people seated near me at the forward end of the car. They seemed to be staring at me curiously. I wondered why I should have attracted their attention. I felt something hot and wet splash on the back of my right wrist.

The birds will rise again in glory, I thought, in 1500 years, when Ravenna and all that it contains shall be sunk from sight beneath the invading sea. I cried without restraint because my heart was breaking.

Getting Funding

'... AND THE TIME is just coming up to eight-twenty-five. We've been talking to Nina Pivonka about her new book, *Caring Parenting While Birding*, this season's runaway success from Backhoe Books, P.O. Box 1885, Caragana, Saskatchewan, Canada's natural publishers. I'm guest host and dramaturge Freddie Poudungian, sitting in this week for Terry. It's time now for our listeners' daily dose of Mozart. This morning it's the Divertimento in D-Major, Koechel 205, about which Einstein speaks so penetratingly.'

CUE MUSIC SEG: MOZART K. 205. 22 MIN

'Back again and hi, everybody. Time eight-forty-seven, and to wind up the final hour on this morning's "Cross Country Arts Admin" on CBCFM we're going to be talking to the paid, full-time director of the spanking-new Junetown Centre for the Creative and Performing Arts, at his office in the rising shell of the building in the complex at the heart of Junetown. Hello Junetown, are you reading me?'

'Clear as a bell, Freddie.'

'Jolly fine, and to start off with, I wonder if you could tell us something about your problems in sub-regional arts planning? This concept of the sub-regional seems to be taking hold among arts officers everywhere. Certainly nobody involved in action in and for the arts has any hangup about dealing with it. At the same time we don't really seem to have a developed understanding of sub-regional problematics. Can you say something about that?'

'Sure can.'   (There is a prolonged on-air wait.)

'Well, go ahead, please.'

'Oh, sorry, well, you see, there's always been all this recognition of your six regions of Canada, the Atlantic provinces, Québec, Ontario, the prairie provinces, B.C., and the north, each of which has its own problematics of identity, see?'

'Yes. I think our listeners are committed to that view of Canada.'

'All well and good, but now we're just beginning to realize that our basic unit of cultural association isn't the region at all; it's the sub-region, or in certain special situations the sub-sub-region, but that's a can of worms we shouldn't open up right at this time. The thing is, if you take Ontario, say, and treat it like one single region, you've backed yourself into a major problem with your concept.'

'Why is that?'

'It's too big. I mean, if Ontario is your basic unit in the arts in this part of Canada, then everybody in Ontario has to be treated like an Ontarian. You can't treat everybody in Africa like an African because they aren't all alike, Egyptians and Moroccans and Yoruba and Boers, and neither are all Ontarians the same. So we're actively emphasizing the local autonomy of the sub-regions and sub-sub-regions, in a few cases. There may be as many as 180 to 200 sub-regions, Etobicoke counts as a sub-region, and then you've got Pickering and the Caledon Hills and Forks of the Credit and the tobacco country and the Lake Erie shore near Dunnville, and the Highlands of Hastings and hundreds more, all with their own culture and problematics.'

'Could you define a problematics for our listeners?'

'A problematics is when you collect all your problems into one.'

'And you're collecting the Junetown problematics?'

'Just defining the parameters, Freddie. I'm becoming deeply involved in our local history and traditions.'

'And you're a native Junetowner?'

'No, actually I'm from Sharbot Lake, but I came to Junetown when I was appointed project manager and I feel like I'd always been here.'

'In the Junetown sub-region?'

'That is correct.'

'I think you've given us a clear idea of what a sub-region is. It might be defined as a place ... a, well, a place. There could be plaques or finger signs pointing it out, from Ontario Heritage.'

'That's perhaps our biggest problem right there, Freddie, to get our people to recognize ourselves as a sub-region like the Highlands of Hastings. There has to be some kind of geographical feature, and there has to be the local history dating back to the middle of the nineteenth century. With us it's the Blue Mountain and the Bally-canoe Road. You see, in the 1870s all the Irishmen around here used to get drunk on Saturday nights and go over to Charleston Village and beat up on the Protestants. That was what they did. We have authentic recreations of this – it's more like a folk festival or myth – in our new ballet "Shillelagh Romp" which was choreo-graphed for us by Anders Svenson.'

'You're going to have a local ballet company?'

'No, no, nothing that ambitious, at least for the first two years, but "Shillelagh Romp" has been shaped to maximize the gifts of untrained indigenous dancers. It takes plenty of rehearsal to mount it, I can tell you.'

'It's in rehearsal already?'

'Yes, at the Tincap Women's Institute Hall. We won't be able to utilize the rehearsal spaces in the new facility for another four to six weeks. After that it will be full speed ahead for the gala opening fortnight of concerts.'

'I'd like to hear a little more about those Ballycanoe Irishmen if I may.'

'There's an abandoned logging road, Freddie, goes into the brush along the east shore of the lake and comes out at Beale's Mills. From there you could take a wagon across country to Charleston Village which was one-hundred-percent Orangemen. That's your dramatic conflict.'

'Orangemen?'

'Orange as orange can be.'

'What are Orangemen?'

'I'm not exactly certain about that, Freddie. Something to do with fruit, I expect. Anyway they're pretty much the bad guys, only the prima ballerina is one of them, only she loves a Ballycanoe boy. There's a pas de deux for them. For the leads, we've been hoping to attract starring dancers from the National Ballet. It's a matter of funding.'

'That's something else we've got to talk about this morning.

You've got a world-class art undertaking on your hands there in Junetown. Can you give us any idea how your costs are going to run and where the money will come from?'

'Got it right here at my fingertips. Our funding sources are the federal and provincial governments, the local municipality, subregional industry and business, and private benefactions. I think any professional in the field would cite those elements of the total package. Naturally in different situations different proportional representation enters into the equation. When you've got a metropolitan municipality behind you, your funding might be figured into the tax rolls and the estimates.'

'But you're not working with a metropolitan nexus.'

'No, that's certainly one strike against us, but then you have to remember the Festival of the Sound, and the Sharon Festival, and the grand success my colleagues are carving out up there in Yellowknife. You see, Freddie, it's an axiom in arts administration that every Canadian citizen is entitled as by right to a full range of arts services, including the drama, concertizing, ethnic dancing, ballet, and oral folk art, with workshops for the potters, carvers and weavers of Canada's first peoples.'

'I see.'

'Now in the case of the Yellowknife initiative you might have fancied that this need was spread pretty thin on the ground. You could spend a whole day – perhaps a whole week – in Yellowknife and never meet a weaver or a potter.'

'Uh-huh.'

'But if they aren't there, you've got to invent them. You've got to get out into the field and dig up those potters. I often think that that's really what a career in arts administration implies, potter-location on a massive scale, and it doesn't just end there. There's the dancers and folk performance artists. And you've got to locate and identify your audience.'

'Wouldn't you do that first?'

'No. You can assume that the audience is out there somewhere, right down to the last seal hunter on the terminal ice-floe. If we have to get right out on the glacier or the tundra, we'll find that woman or man and bring the arts to her or him. She – they – he – whatever – may not feel the need, but the need is always there. I believe that, Freddie, with every fibre of my being.'

'OK, now let's turn our attention to the Junetown sub-region and its audience. Could you tell us exactly how to find Junetown, and what other places are nearby?'

'All you have to do is get yourself onto the 401 headed east from Gananoque and proceed to the Mallorytown exit. Go north on County Road 5, through Mallorytown, and continue approximately three miles further till you come to the Caintown curve. That's where you turn to your left and follow along the road – it's all graded and ready for blacktopping – and in about a mile and a half, not quite two miles, you'll find yourself in the centre of Junetown, and you'll certainly be able to pick out the Junetown Centre for the Creative and Performing Arts.'

'It's easy to spot?'

'Actually it's the only building in the area.'

'But where do the people live?'

'I was hoping you'd ask me that.'

'Well, where do they live?'

'Our sub-region takes in not only Junetown but also Ballycanoe and Caintown, and parts of Quabbin Hill.'

'I see.'

'For example, you'd notice a certain amount of new home construction around Quabbin Hill. It's turning into a suburb of Mallorytown.'

'If you were to draw a circle around Junetown, with a ten-mile radius, how many of our fellow citizens would you take in?'

'How many?'

'That's it.'

'Well, Freddie I don't happen to have the very latest estimates right here, but working from memory and from my own close knowledge of the sub-region ... a ten-mile radius, you say?'

'Ten, fifteen if you like.'

'Oh, now there you'd be including a big chunk of Charleston Lake. In a ten-mile radius, I'd say we're talking eighteen of our fellow arts consumers, and on weekends as many as twenty-one or two.'

'Eighteen?'

'Seven heads of households and from eleven to fifteen dependents, but who's counting?'

'Somebody may be counting. The press may be counting. This is public money after all.'

'It isn't all public money; we have our voluntary contributors.'

'From Quabbin Hill and Caintown?'

'One from each place.'

'Any from Junetown?'

'Not precisely.'

'Does anybody actually live in Junetown?'

'Two people, that's counting me ...'

'... and the other person?'

'... is my lover.'

'I see.'

'We have our rights too, you know, the same rights as any citizen. We've entitled to a share of any money that's going for the arts.'

'I don't think that anybody here on "Cross Country Arts Admin" disputes that, but I do somehow feel that there can't be much demand for "Shillelagh Romp" in Junetown if nobody lives there.'

'But they will live there, once the Centre for the Creative and Performing Arts gets open. We've already sent out over a thousand invitations for the formal opening. The CBC is coming. We expect to see Ian Alexander here for the inside of two full weeks. We've offered to put him up in our own quarters. And you mention the press. I can tell you that press participation has been truly formidable. The publisher of the Stoverville *Intelligencer* has been our strongest supporter. She's been out here almost every morning urging on the workers with shouts of enthusiasm and little kindnesses. She got the Stoverville mobile canteen to put us on its route. Every morning at break time they're here with aid and encouragement and doughnuts. I call it a living testimony and a beacon. As the poet Metcalf is supposed to have said, "To have great poetry, you must have great audiences too." I'll drink to that.'

'And so will I, and so will everybody in CBC arts programming, but you have to have some audience to start with, and on your own showing your audience consists of one loving couple.'

'No, no, nonono, you haven't understood me. We have our satellite communities to draw on. Four families in Caintown and three in Quabbin Hill, not to mention the rural population, which is what we call our floating or transient people-resource.'

'And who are they?'

'We're in process of determining that.'

'And all these people are devoted to the ballet, ethnic and folk dancing, the drama and chamber music?'

'Solid interest has been demonstrated. We have our surveys, you see.'

'I'm sure you have, and on the basis of your surveys you must have made some funding extrapolations. That's really what it's about, isn't it? Can you give us some idea of what all this is going to cost?'

'Freddie, I could recite this in my sleep. We aim to bring the building in at $57 million and change, that's with a full cost-overrun factor. We were originally budgeted at $18 million but that was back in 1986. I think $57 million will stand up.'

'And the operating budget?'

'Ah, now that's where these capital expenditures make a big difference to a sub-region. We expect to have a full-time staff of over seventy people to operate the complex, including maintenance personnel, ticket sales and reservations department, general manager, stage crew, lighting department. The arts and culture create jobs and business opportunities in a community; we should never forget that. Arts spending in Canada is at constantly rising levels of funding, and this makes work.'

'And your funding has been adequate?'

'Well, insofar as funding is ever really adequate to the task, the heavy ongoing task, I think I could give an affirmative to that, but then there's our operating budget to consider. We have to provide for upkeep and operational funding. That's where the township office has been simply magnificent. Almost half the budget of the township of Front of Bastard has been committed to building operation, and it isn't a small sum by any means. The township has promised us close to three-quarters of a million annually over the first five years. It isn't going to be enough, Freddie, not even with our matching grants from the province, but it's one dickens of a start.'

'Nobody would deny that, sir. But I see we're getting close to news time. I think we've got about two minutes remaining. Why not tell us exactly what our fellow citizens can expect for their money during the operation of your facility?'

'It's all right here, Freddie. The building comprises every kind of service area you can think of for arts action. There's the Grand Saloon, that's the concert hall, adaptable for symphony and opera and ballet and major rock stars. Then there's the Petty Saloon, for folk dancing, modern dance, and solo concerts by performance artists and singers, and chamber music. There are a plethora of rehearsal quarters for the various dance companies, and spaces for every kind of dramatic presentation. We have the best cinematic projection equipment, and a state-of-the-technology sound and recording system. The Grand Saloon is going to be an acoustical marvel, they tell me. You'll be able to dine on the banks of scenic Leeder's Slough in your choice of any of six distinctive food-service situations, from economy fast-food and burger service, right through individual, no menu/no visible price list/gourmet wine and food encounters monitored throughout by noted food journalist Joanne Kates. You could imagine yourself voyaging on some ocean greyhound of the period between the wars. And as the twilight lengthens you hear the sound of the strings tuning up as the Caintown Chamber Players prepare to entertain as their guests Liona Boyd, and the Canadian Brass. And so it goes on, this neverending festival carved from the wilderness of southeastern Ontario.

'The main bulk of the building is a stunning harmony in glass and tubing conceived by west-coast architect Tatsumo Hidekaka in the authentic contemporary idiom of Asiatic/Pacific Rim/*style moderne*. So whether you're an art critic or just an ordinary citizen why not plan now to attend the opening summer series of the June-town Centre for the Creative and Performing Arts, amid the wonderland of human involvement with the natural world of rocks and mosses and serpents. Once again, that's the inaugural series at the Junetown Centre. Thank you very much.'

'I think that says it all, listeners. Time now, eight-fifty-nine, or nine-twenty-nine in Newfoundland. This is Freddie Poudungian, sitting in for Terry. We're been talking to the director of the June-town project. Stay tuned for the news, followed by Ken Winters in another of his series of concert re-broadcasts from Salzburg. Good morning.'

CUE: TAPED PROGRAMMING ANNOUNCEMENT. 30 SEC.

'This is the CBC nine o'clock news. I'm Barbara Bunn....'

Third Time Unlucky

WE WENT THERE FIRST exactly two years ago. You might almost say that we were despatched there; we had no specific wish to visit the West Country, apart from a leaning towards ancestor worship which seems to surface in all of us after a certain stage is reached. There were certainly ancestral graves in great numbers laid down in out-of-the-way churchyards along a broad strip of country running from the border of Somerset to the Channel. Odd thing: our forebears on both sides came from thereabouts, as if we'd been destined to meet, long before our lives began. We might be poking around in a cemetery in the very shadow of Maiden Castle, meditating on the antiquities of the site, its mixture of Christian, pre-Christian, Roman, pre-Roman, perhaps pre-Bronze Age, remains, to find among the half-obscured inscriptions of this latter age the surnames of our two paternal lines. They might be names of relative antiquity if considered from the point of view of the living, of perfect novelty if imagined from the angle conferred by the earthworks of Maiden Castle, an edifice of immeasurable age, whose builders could not have imagined the incursions of suburban Dorchester, tiles and drains and commodious brick dwellings and modern cemeteries, on defences built to exclude tribes so ancient that their names have gone unrecorded.

'There have been creatures like us in these parts for a long long time,' said Irene one slanting afternoon as we picked our way out of the churchyard at Winterbourne Abbas to meet the bus to Bridport. 'Put a finger into the mud and you unearth an axe and a bone, sinister collocation.' She gave me a sidelong grin. 'Strange that our two families should lie so near one another.'

'Coincidence is the only really active principle in human life,' I said slowly. 'Wasn't it Thomas Hardy who celebrated "Hap" in some poem or other? Pure accident, chance or mischance. Obscure coming-together ostensibly intended by nobody. The reflection

31

seems inevitable, as we can't be more than a few miles from the writer's place of birth.'

'Place of death too, I believe,' said Irene, scraping mould from her small shoes as we approached the bus stop. 'Wasn't he buried not far from his birthplace?'

'Only his heart.'

'Where's the rest of him?'

'In the Abbey. They removed the heart and buried it between the graves of his two wives.'

'How very macabre!'

I was compelled to agree. Then the bus appeared; the driver stopped most courteously to pick us up some few hundred feet from the appointed stop. Tumuli and long barrows lay on either side of the carriageway, easily identified in their dress of fresh green. The bus lurched forward, gathered speed, then began the long ascent to Askerswell where the wind blows forever across the weathered roof of a solitary motel, little patronized in summer and in winter as wholly uninhabited by the living as Maiden Castle itself. The activities of very early men and women show themselves everywhere from this high point; they lie around and below the site in their shadowy dwellings in surprising numbers. I suppose they have their comings and their goings too.

Half an hour brought us down the reverse slope of the A-35 into Bridport, used by us as a base because of its Hardyesque associations and its persistence in family record on either side. Until quite recently there was a rail service from Maiden Newton to Bridport which linked Dorchester to West Dorset, but invisible powers had their wilful way with the little branch line, and the rail connection is no more. You can see where it used to be if you pay a visit to Maiden Newton station, but there are no traces of the line where it used to enter Bridport.

Irene is no lover of bus transport, considering it plebeian, unlucky, unworthy of the attention of elevated spirits, too tightly scheduled to allow for any free play of "hap" or impulse. Superior beings ought to be free to come and go as they wish; schedules impose a disagreeable familiarity upon travellers. You keep seeing the same faces: the woman who boards the 95 bus every morning in Lyme Regis to ride two stops up the hill towards Uplyme, admittedly a steep walk, yet one which might do much to check her threatened obesity. The man with the small smooth-haired terrier, whose obscure family relationship with the morning driver has earned his terrier a prescriptive right to certain liberties.

The little doggie used to sniff his way along the aisle of the bus, testing ankles and stockings for acceptability, gazing up earnestly at the place where Irene and I usually sat, his small face creased in puzzlement as if he – or perhaps she – couldn't quite make us out. I used to find the sight of this confusion faintly amusing – the animals are as frequently confused by instinct as ourselves. The dog's owner would issue a benign command, then the two of them would debouch from the bus at their customary point of descent. That whole route is little more than a means of cosy local association. We grew to recognize many of its riders between Bridport and Lyme and Axminster or Chard, almost the familiar spirits of those places.

'This morning, Chris, this morning we'll go over to Axminster and catch the train to Exeter, go over the cathedral – there are some remarkable memorials – and catch the bus back from Axminster in time to be in Bridport before dinner. How does that strike you?'

I've learned to acquiesce in Irene's impulses. I often think that she responds more fully to the possibilities of random motive than I. It's important to move around spontaneously; one never knows what may happen. We did as she suggested, arriving at the railway station in Axminster in good time to catch a train connection to Exeter, where we examined the two railway stations and the cathedral before attempting a heavy cream tea not really very long after the hour of luncheon. In the cathedral we located a memorial tablet sacred to the memory of Lt.-Gen. John Graves Simcoe, which enshrined him as a local notable but made no mention of his one immense historical action, the founding of the great city of Toronto. How quickly does the heroic undertaking of the past lapse into the sea of the unrecorded.

We passed some time in buzzing about the ears of one of the cathedral clergymen, impressing upon him the necessity of revising the delinquent tablet or replacing it by one which included more appropriate wording. The expression of surprise which fled across the face of this poor dean, archdeacon, canon or whatever he was – he wore a long white gown in some indifferent stuff, with red bands around the shoulders – lasted us all the way across the cathedral green and into a neighbouring tea-shop, where we assumed the guise of innocent travellers in need of sweet refreshment. Sitting in the window of the tea-shop, barricaded behind mounds of stiff cream, we noticed the dean or archdeacon standing in the porch looking round him in bewilderment.

'When next we come here, we'll have to follow up the resurrection of poor Simcoe's name,' said Irene.

'Next time?'

'Chris, you're so slow! Finish up your jam, there's a good child, and we'll make for the station. We don't want to miss the bus from Axminster.'

'I ate too much in there.'

'You can relax on the train.' And as usual she was right. I stared reflectively at the wet, intensely green fields of Devon as the admirable train ran swiftly through them. At Axminster there was a brief moment of repose; then at the appointed hour the bus for Bridport, Dorchester and Weymouth appeared in the station yard, virtually empty. It was five minutes to six, which allowed us a forty-five-minute ride and a brisk ten-minute walk to our hotel. We sat back and prepared to make ourselves invisible, bent on observation of our fellow passengers, and whatever natural phenomena presented themselves. We ground and rattled noisily up the hill out of Axminster, looking carefully around the bus; we were almost alone in the vehicle. Only the driver, penned into his forward compartment by the fare box and a small swinging gate, an elderly woman burdened with two sizeable straw carryalls, and a timid-seeming man in a neat blue suit shared the rather dingy interior.

'I think that's our man,' giggled Irene, giving me at the same moment a sharp dig in the ribs. She indicated the man in the blue suit as a possible target for agreeable conversation. We make it our business to speak to as many of the locals as time and politeness allow. We've often made peculiar discoveries in this way. Irene turned right round in our seat, so as to be able to take a sight of our fellow passenger. She seemed about to speak to him, had indeed enunciated an introductory syllable or two, when suddenly the bus emitted a series of protesting noises which filled the air like pistol shots, dispelling the pleasant stillness of the end of the afternoon. Engine noise ceased at once. The bus, moving on a slight up-grade in the direction of Uplyme, came gradually to a careful halt on the left shoulder of the roadway. The driver applied his emergency brake, setting the lever in an extreme position, and turned around to address us in some embarrassment.

'Gearbox is gone,' he said succinctly, with a distinct West Dorset intonation. 'I've been expecting this to happen any day.' He seemed pleased to have his expectations confirmed. The blue-suited man looked uneasily from side to side without giving tongue. The woman with the heavy carryalls at once manifested grave unease which seemed only partly dispelled by our driver's nonchalant manner.

'Fowerty years on this service I've been,' he declared, 'and 'tis the first time this has happened to me. Drove my bus along blacked-out lanes with my lamps switched off during the bombings, and never an accident. And now this.' He paused. 'There isn't the maintenance. And due to retire next week and going to America.'

'But what shall we do?' demanded the woman with the straw bags, rotating herself stiffly in her seat.

'Naught to do but wait. I'd best walk along to the pub in Uplyme and telephone from there. Relief bus from Bridport in half an hour or thereabouts.' He worked the door open with some difficulty. 'No air pressure, do you see? I'sll come back at once and wait with you.'

'It's no great distance to the Goat and Compasses,' said the man in the blue suit, breaking his silence. 'Matter of five minutes, either way.' He addressed himself to the women. 'No need to be alarmed, ma'am. We shall be home well before dark.'

'I've two frozen chickens in here,' said she, giving the larger bag a shake. All at once she began to laugh. 'Happen nothing will go amiss with them, for they won't thaw in an hour.'

After this homely remark, conversation became general. Irene offered some remarks on the preparation of poultry for the table, to which the woman replied with accounts of her experiences with ducks. I stole a careful look at the man behind us and decided that this would be an appropriate moment to say something to him. He stood up and moved several paces forward along the aisle, finally seating himself in a position immediately behind us.

'Just to be companionable-like,' he said, with a pleading air of uncertainty in his movements. When I said something to him this uncertainty seemed to dissolve. I spoke with a North American accent, therefore I could not be identified with any local class or group, was plainly not one of the local nobs. He smiled, looking directly at me for the first time. I don't know what he saw, but there was a wavering alarm in his eyes. Had he been right to speak to us familiarly? He seemed deeply unsure.

He was a person of the office-worker class, in late middle age, with smoothly combed brown hair receding slightly at the parting above the right temple. There were traces of dandruff at the hair-line, which was disciplined into immobility by some hair dressing or oil, which smelt faintly of lemon. His forehead was ridged in three rolls or creases, and in repose displayed two deep horizontal lines and the small bracketed vertical lines between the eyebrows which suggest an habitual squint. The whites of his eyes were slightly reddened, perhaps by working in an ill-ventilated room where others regularily smoked, perhaps from being out in severe weather. He wore a shirt of fairly good quality, but not of cotton alone, with a pale salmon-coloured ground and a faint brown stripe. His necktie was knotted rather loosely. He wore a light blue knitted sleeveless pullover under the jacket of a suit made of excellent serge not very well cut. There was a small row of pens and pencils visible in the left breast pocket next his lapel, and the badge of some club or fraternal organization in the buttonhole of the opposite lapel. His expression seemed one of forced geniality mixed with anxiety, per-haps connected with his physical condition which suggested poor nourishment. I thought I detected a faint bluish tinge at the edge of the lower lip.

'We'll be home late tonight,' he said, attempting cheerfulness. He seemed about to offer me a cigarette, but I shook my head in what I suppose was a kind of feigned withdrawal. Blue smoke rose in the air. 'Getting on,' he said. I nodded silently. We heard the cheery voice of the driver behind us, as he clambered back into the stuffy interior.

'Relief bus along in thirty minutes,' he said loudly. 'Would any lady or gentlemen care for a slice of Turkish delight?' When nobody accepted this unlooked-for invitation he took a silver-wrapped oblong from the remains of a packed lunch, unpeeled it, blew away the floury sugar which whitened the contents, and ate it with an air of liberated informality.

''Twas the wife's favourite for more than fowerty year,' he said. Chat grew free and spontaneous. The driver was about to embark on a new post-retirement life, beginning at the end of the next week with a long-anticipated visit to his children and grandchildren in 'America'. We were unable to draw from him the precise location of the visit. His destination was plainly conceivable to him as a vast romantic undifferentiated space, something like Heaven.

The quiet lady passenger revealed doubts about a bit of steak which she had left out on top of the Aga. Might it not begin to spoil if she were late in returning? Irene reassured her on the point. 'Decomposition commences much more slowly in animal flesh than we suppose,' she said. 'Your meat will remain whole and agreeable to the taste for at least another eighteen hours. Not to worry.'

The woman smiled gratefully at this news, which I personally would have received as somewhat off-putting. Irene is like that, precise to a degree. I think her observations on the normal rate of putrefaction made our other companion uneasy. He shifted in his seat, bent his head towards me confidentially and whispered in my ear.

'Your missus?'

'And a co-worker,' I said.

'Very knowledgeable lady, she seems.'

'She has a remarkable fund of information,' I said.

'Aye, that's where I could wish to enjoy her companionship,' he said, 'or, pardon me, the companionship of someone like her. I need a better memory, do you see? I'm the local insurance collector. I travel up and down from Weymouth to Taunton, receiving the monthly premiums and trying to sell new policies. I tell them, I say, that insurance is their best bet; you can't lose by it for we're all going to die at some time or other. It's the only certain wager.'

'Everybody knows old Robin,' said the bus-driver merrily, 'and some calls him the death-watch beetle.'

'Oh, go on,' said the steak and chickens lady, laughing unwillingly.

Matters had gone on in much this way for another twenty minutes when a second blue bus, much newer and smarter in turnout than the first, appeared over the ridge above Uplyme and pulled around in a difficult U-turn so that it was headed in the proper direction. Our original driver transferred his cashbox and ticket dispenser, his jacket and the remains of the Turkish delight, into the driver's seat of the relief vehicle, leaving his mate to oversee the recovery of the broken-down machine. Soon we were bowling down the steep descent into Lyme, where the lady of the uncooked beefsteak left us with a contented smile. She hurried away up a steep side street, relief evident in every line of her frame. Then we began the slow climb up the eastern approach to the town where, halfway to the top, we could see the vast bulk of Golden Cap reflecting orange-red in the last sun.

'Makes you think solemn thoughts, does that noble view,' murmured the man in blue. 'Nearly home now.' When we were back on the main roadway he stood up in the aisle, balancing awkwardly and rocking with the motion of the bus. He assembled his belongings carefully. I saw a fat volume of actuarial tables protruding from a bulging briefcase. Papers fell from his pockets. I picked some of them up, noticing the name of a celebrated insurance firm at their head, and handed them to him. As he began to thank me the bus slowed to a halt somewhere between Charmouth and Chideock, at a concealed lane entry.

'I'll let you down here, my lad,' said the driver, 'special service for season ticket holders, you see, as we're so late.' The doors hissed open, the man descended, turned and gave us a last friendly smile, then disappeared into a nearby grove of trees and shrubs.

'Miles older than you'd think, is Robin,' said the driver. 'Known him since I was in the forces. Nineteen forty-three that was, and old Robin was collecting for the Royal Liverpool then. But there, I suppose he earns a living by it.'

He drove rapidly away, dropping us at a convenient point in Bridport perhaps forty minutes behind schedule. When we entered the dining room of our hotel later than was customary, our genial host was quick to register surprise. 'About ready to send the dogs out,' he said, 'but here you are then, all safe.' We began to eat voraciously.

Neither Irene nor I paid further attention to the incident of the broken-down bus until business and pleasure dictated a second visit to the identical locality at the same season last year. We had gone early in the morning along the same bus route from Bridport to the unromantic, not-very-often-visited townsite of Chard. There we found a taxi driver with whom we arranged a visit to the wildlife sanctuary at Cricket Saint-Thomas. Irene is fascinated by the larger forms of wildlife, the bigger cats and apes, while I can never resist the cages of exotic, splendidly-coloured birds from every quarter of the globe ... like so many human souls illuminated in the glory of their passing. I expect to oversee their arrival in the next world. We gazed and gazed: panthers and elephants and jerboas and blue-footed boobies and chattering lories. A meat tea in the new café. Almost too promptly our taxi returned in the middle of our tea to take us back to Chard, and we quitted the wide valley with reluctance, a bit too slowly as things turned out. We missed the four o'clock bus and had to kill forty-five minutes in the crowded uninteresting town, wondering as we paced about why the gutters of Chard ran eternally with water, as if fed from some nearby sacred fount. Investigation of the course of the flow helped somewhat to pass the time.

I bought the current number of *Country Life* and took it along onto the bus with me. We left town towards five p.m. with a long run ahead of us through Axminster and Lyme and so home. I buried myself in *Country Life*, examining blurred photographs of some very hauntworthy old houses, when after several jerky stops Irene seized me by the shoulder and whispered, 'Look there, do you see, Chris? It's him. He.'

'Who?'

'The man who was with us on the bus last year, when it broke down and we were so late for our meal. It was a year ago almost to the day.'

I stared at the person whom she pointed out, sitting across the aisle, several seats in front of us this time. I was uncertain for a moment and then the man turned and I saw his left profile. She was perfectly right. There was a small wart or mole on the cheek just below the ear, which I'd noticed the previous year. Same mole; same man. 'Talk about coincidence,' she muttered in my ear. We decided not to call ourselves to his attention, fearing to alarm him or engage ourselves in a tedious and consciously misleading explanation of our reappearance.

By unspoken consent we shrank down into our seats so as to minimize visibility, perhaps even causing ourselves to disappear altogether. From this constricted space we spied on our man as he shifted warily in his place, now and then turning his head and shoulders like a suspicious deer, as if some unbidden recollections were forcing their way into his consciousness. He wore the same suit as before, a trifle more worn and shiny in appearance. I could see a thickish scattering of fallen dandruff on his shoulders; he might be in poorer health than before. Once he turned right round and stared the length of the bus as if he thought he was being followed.

Unable to resist such a suggestion, Irene began to act out a role in some imaginary film concerned with espionage or gangsterism. She pulled her smart felt hat well down over her eyes, squinted menacingly at our quarry, gazing fiercely at the nape of his puffy neck as if attempting to force an entry to his very mind or soul by some preternatural persuasion. Once she formed the shape of a tiny blowgun with her left hand, aimed it at the base of her target's skull and blew briskly down the imagined tube as though she launched a poisoned dart. 'Whssshhttt.' Her enactment of the assassin's role was curiously persuasive.

Poor Robin's uneasiness increased visibly. It was clear soon enough that he had somehow become aware of our presence, for as the bus went past the point where we had come to an untoward halt the year before, he turned and spoke to us, rather discomfiting us by the suddenness of the address. 'Do you see the pub yonder, the Goat and Compasses? That's where our driver called in for relief last year.'

We supplied a disingenuous explanation of our return to the neighbourhood.

'Well, I'm right glad to see you,' said the life insurance man, 'it was the inn sign as made me recollect you. Goat and compasses. Do you know what that was before Cromwell's times? God Encompasseth Us. Had to be washed away and changed utterly, too papistical and foreign and too prayerful-like.'

''Twould be wicked indeed to be too prayerful-like,' said Irene. I could feel her shaking with unexpressed mirth.

'Since our forced halt of a year ago, I've always said a short prayer of thanksgiving when passing that place,' said old Robin. 'It could have been so much worse. Our brakes might have failed at the top of the incline; then we'd have careered down into Lyme with no means of a stop. We might have killed some poor body.'

'Or perhaps some little doggie,' I said.

Our driver glanced back and joined the conversation. Now there were only four of us in the vehicle. He spoke with bitterness. 'I can think of some little doggies would profit by being run over by this bus.'

He was a new young driver, not at all the same type of man as our previous chauffeur, now presumably safe in the bosom of family connections in America. This driver had a narrow face and generally vulpine air. 'The busman's curse,' he muttered, 'little doggies.'

We ran through Lyme without incident, our exchange of talk with the man in blue serge growing intermittent and inconsequential. Then in a moment, chance, 'hap', coincidence, reared its astonishing head. We had come down a long slope and could not have been more than five miles from our destination, when our bus came urgently to a halt. The roadway was entirely blocked by a sizeable tractor-trailer which was lodged at right angles across the pavement, apparently immovable. It was immediately clear what had happened. Its driver had tried to execute a full right-angled turn in reverse, so as to manoeuvre his trailer onto a gravelled drive which led up through a clump of trees towards a large dwelling partly concealed by foliage.

An ill-judged turning angle, and a loosely packed gravel shoulder at the gateway, had caused the heavily laden trailer to slip sideways into a deep and wide ditch. The coupling between tractor and trailer was now so strained that the front wheels of the tractor were off the ground; the driving wheels at the rear of the tractor were up to their hubs in heavy mud and loose stones. Parts of the load lay here and there in the damp ditch.

'I can't believe this,' said our acquaintance. 'Twice on the same date, at the same time of day.' He goggled at us in disbelief, while I attempted to produce a rational explanation of what could only be raw coincidence.

'Coincidence,' he expostulated, as Irene slid out of our seat and stood looking down at him in the friendliest way. 'Naw, naw, that's what I calls fate, that is.'

He might almost have suspected us of having planned the incident, which was certainly troublesome enough. We were delayed for close to two hours this time, with a line of evening traffic lengthening behind us and a corresponding line stretching off in the other direction. When an army hoist-vehicle appeared on the scene its operators could hardly make their way to the accident site through the press of idling motors and vans and the crowds of cursing drivers. There were no cheers and congratulatory embraces when the wrecked commercial vehicle was finally dragged from the mire, much of its load – office equipment, stationery, photocopying machines – distributed in deep mud. When our companion left the bus at a stop somewhere near Chideock, his features were grey with fatigue and half-formed suspicion.

So that this afternoon, another year later to the day and the hour, when we entered the bus for a conclusive ride from Axminster to Bridport, we didn't reveal ourselves at once. Sure enough our man climbed into the bus, seated himself with a furtive air, and looked around the interior with care. He wasn't to see us though. He looked very much older, and we remembered that he had been peddling life insurance hereabouts for almost fifty years. Time runs out on all of us sooner or later, doesn't it? Though we knew he was our friend of the two previous runs, we resolved to remain hidden unless some incredible further coincidence asserted itself.

We passed the Goat and Compasses, looking at one another with smiles, remembering poor Robin's apocryphal derivation of the name. God encompasseth us, indeed! Down into Lyme without incident. Up the other side of the long dip, Golden Cap grey today and hard to make out through gathering fog. Back onto the A-35 and picking up speed, only four of us along for the ride, the driver, the passenger, and us. Through Charmouth. Through Chideock. Very close to old Robin's home. Then without warning the driver swerved wildly to avoid an animal, most probably a dog, which chose that moment to scamper across the carriageway. The bus lurched from side to side as the driver guided it expertly up an overgrown lane into a clutch of underbrush. The tips of shrubbery branches scraped along the rows of windows like the fingers of the buried dead. We rose from our seats and advanced towards our familiar companion. Behind him the driver barred his way of escape. His face worked convulsively as though he beheld a pair of terrible spectres. 'It's you, it's you,' he cried out, in the grip of mortal fear, and he made as though to turn for the emergency exit, but before he could do anything to save himself we were upon him.

Deanna and the Ayatollah

IT IS AN ALMOST TOTALLY UNKNOWN FACT of contemporary history that the adorable and idolized star of twenty-two movie musicals, Deanna Durbin, and the even more celebrated insurgent chief of the Shiite Moslems, the Ayatollah Ruhollah Khomeini, lived next door to one another in the tiny French village of Neauphle-le-château some twelve miles west of Paris, for several years preceding the Islamic leader's return to his native country towards the end of the seventies.

Neauphle-le-château was for generations an insignificant farming community, then briefly a town centre and market for the produce of the surrounding farms, finally a bedroom suburb of Paris. It came to resemble those small centres on the New Haven trackage northeast of New York along the shores of the Sound, retreats for media personalities who like to live close to the production centres, at the same time enjoying certain of the pleasures of country retreat, factitious anonymity, the mask of obscurity, grateful exile from the bright lights.

Now it happens that Miss Durbin began her life in the production centres at an excessively young age – she was a perfectly genuine instance of the child star. All the rest of her life she has been much younger than her long time before the public would suggest. She chose retirement as long ago as 1949 when she was still almost a young girl, still in her mid-twenties. But the unforgettably charming woman with the best voice of all the film stars (the sweetest, the truest, the best-disciplined, the best-produced) still seems in her rare public appearances to be young, young, forever the lovely child of *One Hundred Men and a Girl*, in which she was supported by another performer of incredible durability, Leopold Stokowski. No doubt association with Stokowski helped to prepare the young singer for an infinitely more tricky and surprising collaboration with a person who closely resembled him physically, and in other ways too.

Anyway, when Deanna quitted the cinema and the shores of North America forever she was still almost a girl. She still possessed the unlined eager face and the determined, authoritative nature which made it easy for her to say to her friends in the business, 'Enough. No more. I'm through!'

She had had two husbands and was about to take a third, as things turned out the right man, a rich, clever, extremely intelligent Frenchman who had been one of Renoir's assistants and afterwards director of Deanna's best-looking film, *Lady on a Train*, over which the influences of Renoir and Welles brood like guardian spirits. *Lady on a Train* is a wonderful-looking picture, painterly in its chiaroscuro, very French in its wit. Like all of Miss Durbin's movies it appeals much more to European sensibilities than to American. We must never forget that Deanna was Winston's favourite star. In the bunker in the Blitz he would cause her films to be run and re-run, chuckling over them, sometimes shedding a tear. Her person was and remains almost overpoweringly appealing. But when she came to the age of twenty-seven, when she had grown tired of the cruel demands of the film star's existence, she showed something which none but her closest friend might have suspected: iron determination and the courage that never takes a backward step.

She married; she lived for a while in Switzerland; she bore children and raised them very far from the madding crowd. She didn't have any more husbands; this time she'd gotten the correct one. And in the course of years this rich and happy family came to settle near Paris, to enjoy the unfolding of one another's lives, the secure intelligent pretty children with their little birds' voices and their slanting European eyes, the wise talented father, the strong gifted mother. They had a few close friends and they gave select evening parties, at which Deanna sang much more difficult and musically interesting pieces than she ever delivered on the screen. She worked with the best available coaches. She sang the songs of Duparc and Fauré; she sang lieder. She exercised her voice with Handel and learned the part of the Countess in *Figaro*. She might have made a meltingly beautiful Mozart singer. Now and then she read over the appropriate roles in Gilbert and Sullivan and their musical wit always made her choke with laughter. Paris lay near; the family was very rich; she approached her forties.

And then one day, walking in her extensive grounds, near the wall which shielded her from prying representatives of the media, those killers who had destroyed her friend and early colleague Judy Garland not very long before, she saw signs of activity in the near neighbouring gardens. Just on the other side of her shielding wall some remarkable figures seemed to be coming and going. They seemed to be covertly inspecting her, so far as she could tell from the glimpses she obtained by standing on tiptoe and occasionally jumping up and down. When she jumped up and down she exhibited much of the irresistible little-girl's charm which had brought her so quickly to world fame twenty-five years before. A mouth-watering woman.

There were lots of men behind the wall, all dressed in black, in what looked – though this could scarcely be possible – like *robes*. Who could tell what might be concealed under that sober raiment? Plastic explosive perhaps. Automatic weaponry. It was a time of distressful conflict in Paris and these strange figures unquestionably had an Arabian air. Algerian dissidents?

But that could hardly be. Algeria had gained independence some years before under an ingenious settlement which only the great Charlie could have achieved. France, the home of political liberty, willing host to revolutionaries of every kind, had disembarrassed herself of the Algerian question. Why should men in black robes come to trouble the tranquillity of M et Mme Charles David, who only wished to be at peace with everyone and to preserve an uninterrupted privacy?

Ah, Deanna, somebody who wished even more than you to be private had moved in next door, somebody in an unexceptionable lounge suit, not in robes at all. A man with a thin triangular face, deeply-sunken cheeks and magnificent eyes, who plainly stood at the centre of this crowd of Arabs. As he came and went in the walled garden next door, this man was followed and deferred to by his menacing swarm of retainers. A phrase which she had never before needed or even dared to think went through the lady's head. Security men, she said to herself. She hurried inside to talk matters over with her husband.

'My dearest, these are very extensive gardens; there isn't the smallest need for us to enter into any relationship with these people. They may not even speak French.'

'Oh, but they do. I heard them addressing the servants. And they speak other languages too, which I couldn't recognize.'

'They spoke no English?'

'Oh, no, no! I don't believe any of them know English. Somehow I don't think they would want to speak English, certainly not American English.'

Deanna retained some emotional ties with America, certainly never identified the continent as the Great Satan, though she had no wish to revisit it at any time.

'Should we redouble our security precautions?'

'My angel, I think that you will find these men even more conscious of security than we are.'

Something in her husband's look and gestures reassured the star, at the same time exciting her curiosity.

'Do you know something you haven't told me?' she demanded.

Her husband crossed the spacious *salon* to where she stood. When he took her magnificent arm a sharp spark of static electricity passed between them, generated by the rubbing of excellent leather over Aubusson. These small shocks were the price one paid for *grande luxe.*

'I believe their leader to be a king in exile.'

Deanna breathed more quickly. Her bosom rose and fell in excitement and her husband felt the familiar thrill of sexual adoration. It is something indeed to pass your life in the company of one of the most beautiful and famous women in the world. Every day film and television and recording producers tried to communicate with M et Mme Charles David, hoping to entice the star from retirement. All over the world people wanted to know whether Deanna had retained her glorious innocence, her sweet, bell-like tones. Charles David thought of the miserable death of Judy Garland as he clung to his wife's plump rounded forearm. The world must do without its darling!

'A king in exile,' he repeated, and his wife shivered with delicious excitement. Once or twice she had appeared in films set more or less in Ruritania. Who could tell what plans were being laid on the other side of those high protective walls?

She pouted. She said, 'The walls are there to protect *us*.'

'It can do no harm if they protect our neighbours as well.'

'And we need have nothing to do with them?'

'Exactly!'

Now when she perambulated her formal gardens, which extended through many hectares, as she passed slowly through beech groves and picked her way around ancient oaks, the scent of hawthorn intoxicating in the languorous summer air, Deanna often felt a curious, unlooked-for pique. Here was she, the sought-after, the adored, reclusive in her celebrated retirement, and these folk next door seemed to feel no need to draw closer to her. This constituted a troubling rearrangement of natural priorities and she resented it.

She planned and carried out a series of evening recitals at which the leading Parisian executants of chamber music and art song performed for a select guest list. Crystal chandeliers sparkled, throwing their starry light over parterre and gardens. Famous ladies and their cavaliers consumed ices on the terraces. Hollywood producers schemed in the *seizième* for invitations to these musical evenings and were regularly refused admission to the household when their stiff invitation cards were revealed as not-very-ingenious forgeries. Hired limos drifted soundlessly back to Paris, housing studio biggies and their muttered discontents. Naturally this *va-et-vient* made the folks next door wonder what was up. In the still courts of the charismatic leader, the repository of the hopes of a vital, turbulent religious movement of immense power and resource, the lights and the music, the splendid ladies and the courtly gentlemen, their jewels, their linen, must have seemed the acme of frivolity. The bell-like voice that was so often lifted up in stunning aria seemed alien, enchanting, mysterious, intolerably attractive, like the Divine presence in Sufi mystical verse. The Ayatollah took to walking slowly in his garden, perhaps – who can tell – hoping to scrape some sort of acquaintance with such a singer.

The Ayatollah Ruhollah Khomeini had not at this time – when he was already an old man of seventy-two or three – taken on his shoulders the full burden of worldwide celebrity which Deanna Durbin had been forced to bear from childhood. That image of the terrifying opposer of all things Western, the enemy of the counter-revolutionary trashiness of the consumer society, had not yet taken shape in anyone's imagination. If you had passed him on the street, say in Paris or London, at that period, you could easily have taken the Ayatollah for one of those professors or lifelong students who haunt the Western capitals in pursuit of private learning, students perhaps of the philosophy of Avicenna, Averroes or Avicebron, self-exiled in Paris where wonderful libraries of mediaeval philo-sophical thought have been preserved. Such a man might be an astronomer or a mathematician, might haunt Bloomsbury and the Museum for fifty years, clad in an ill-fitting blue or gray suit, slip-ping around corners near Bedford Square, staying out of the pubs. Lean yellowish-grey hungry-looking imageless men.

Beech leaves swirled around his slippers; he moved soundlessly nearer the high barrier. A wind began to rise in the tall poplars; soon the autumn rains would begin. A pre-condition of the status of ruler-in-exile is the constant tormenting sense that something of final importance is going to happen ... but just when? It is impossi-ble to say for certain. The Ayatollah tried to see over the wall, and one fine day towards the end of October he and Deanna jumped in the air at the same moment. Each saw the other's face flash at the top of the wall, then fall away. The Ayatollah did not insist on the use of the *chador*, its binding imposition on women, when he was in Paris, realizing like a wise man that the custom was unacceptable there. He felt pleased to catch a glimpse of this person, and mixed with the pleasure, he suddenly became aware, was an extraordinary impulse to advance upon her, to know her. Great beauty makes us move towards itself. The greater the beauty the swifter the inclination. He would have to be very careful of his conduct, said the Ayatollah Ruhollah Khomeini to himself. He instructed his bodyguard to find out all they could about the people on the other side of the wall. Imagine his consternation when he found himself to be the next-door neighbour of a film star, and what was worse, a film star who had fled from the embrace of her adorers. Some sort of parable about worship and adoration was implied in her history. He resolved to know her better, and began to keep track of her appearances in the garden. It was not difficult to arrange an encounter.

Ordering his security staff to remain indoors, sure that he had little to fear, he proceeded to stroll down his customary pathway towards the great shade trees, carrying with him a bundle of scrolled sheets of fine paper. He could see the top of the lady's head over the wall. She seemed to be wearing some sort of elaborate headdress. A late-autumn breeze sprang up from a convenient quarter and the Ayatollah released as though accidentally some of the papers which he carried. They bore a series of trivial communications in Arabic script, in fact a group of prayer formulae which a film-star would naturally be unable to read. The long sheets of paper fluttered into the air and he guided them expertly over the wall, at the same time crying out loudly in French as though confounded at their accidental flight. He heard exclamations of womanly excitement from over the wall and he cried out again as if in despair. There came crunching and scraping sounds from the neighbouring garden. In a moment the top of a sturdy aluminium ladder came into view and seconds later the head and shoulders of Deanna Durbin at fifty. Khomeini was transfixed. Even at fifty this woman exerted a fascination the like of which he had never experienced. He tried to mutter a sacred ejaculation, the central utterance of Islamic worship, but suddenly he saw that the prayer was unnecessary. There is no God but God. He eyed the woman uneasily and retreated a step. She perceived the movement of retreat at once, and her heart warmed to the poor stranger. What did she see? A thin, short, half-starved, hollow-cheeked old man with a stubble and a stoop. Her superb natural disposition spoke before she could restrain herself.

'I'm having a few friends in for music, *une très petite soirée*, this evening, and I wondered if you might care to be present. We have pictures which you would enjoy seeing.' She knew nothing of the Ayatollah's iconoclasm; at the beginning of the seventies he didn't stress the breaking up of images. He liked to examine Western paintings, mainly of the School of Paris, while sipping a glass of punch, as well as the next man. He went alone to Deanna's *soirée*, leaving strict instructions to his guards that if he hadn't returned by one in the morning they were to attack the neighbouring house with automatic weapons and liberate him.

The rescue action proved unnecessary. No enemy agents lay in wait for him in the splendid lady's home. There were present her husband, tall, charming, hospitable, and their attractive children and, as Deanna had promised, a very few friends who practised a rich, knowing tact, making no overtures to the poor Arab. Instead they came and went in the shadows, whispering together their enjoyment of the music, the paintings, the *boiseries*. It was the Ayatollah's first taste of luxury; he had sometimes enjoyed comfort, often slept in adequate beds, always alone. He had never wallowed in sensory delight. It came to him in uplifting waves of pleasure-shock.

From that time on he saw a lot of Deanna; they became intimates, and he was even able to reveal something of his political situation. The administration of the Shah Reza Pahlavi was tottering; it had enemies everywhere in Europe and the Near and Middle East. Its terrible secret police, who had made a refined art of torture and murder, were hated from Libya to Pakistan, most of all in Iran itself. Only American military assistance and American intelligence operations remained to prop up this collapsing régime. The Pahlavi were not an ancient house; their reign dated back no more than fifty years in Persian history. They were the merest adventurers and possessed nothing of the true faith.

'But Ayatollah dear,' crooned Deanna, 'you aren't nearly ready to take power.'

This conversation took place somewhere about 1974 or 1975, when American power and policy were in tatters following upon the humiliations of the Watergate affair. Even Miss Durbin, who knew nothing about the foreign or domestic policies of America, knew by some artist's instinct that matters might soon draw to a head. She liked the Ayatollah very much; he was a quiet accommodating neighbour. At her request, he had dismissed, or at least made much less visible, his corps of security officers.

'I've enough security for two,' said Deanna. 'No harm can come to you when Deanna is near.' What she said comforted the old man. She was an endless repository of sound counsel, having much to teach him.

'You don't have an impressive figure. You're too short and too thin. I don't suppose you'd remember, my dear, but in the mid-thirties when I was starting my career, Walt Disney had two characters in his Mickey Mouse stories who looked like they were developing into something, Clarabelle Cow and Horace Horsecollar.'

The Ayatollah listened with rapt attention.

'The studio gave them every chance to evolve. They had distinctive costumes. They had *lines*.'

He nodded attentively.

'But Ruhollah dear, they simply didn't have image. They didn't register on the screen, so of course when Donald Duck came along they just faded into nothing, and we never hear about them nowadays. You don't want to be a Clarabelle Cow.'

The Ayatollah shuddered.

'And then,' she went on, 'after the first success of Donald Duck, who made a strong impression on his fans, there were the usual rip-offs, as my children would describe them. Usually a rip-off doesn't do as well as the original, but in this case the rip-off lasted longer and had a more important career than the original. Mine didn't. None of the Deanna imitations lasted six months: Gloria Jean, Kathryn Grayson, Patricia Morison. But when *Daffy* Duck came along ... well ... he had chemistry. He had insouciance. He had *flair*.'

She paused for a moment, deep in thought.

'I think it was the blackness,' she said finally, 'the way his eyes and his bill were wrapped in mystery, in a surround of black.' She squinted at the Ayatollah. 'You know,' she said, 'there's a bit of Daffy in you, around the nose and eyes. Here, just a minute.' She seized a black shawl or throw which lay on the piano and draped it over the unresisting religious leader's head and shoulders.

'My dear, it's you,' she said, and she led him to a magnificent crystal looking-glass. The Ayatollah looked at himself in the glass and was pleased with what he saw. The black robe certainly did a lot for him. It gave him a subtle mystery.

'Whiskers,' said Deanna, 'sideburns, let them grow. Take off another five pounds. You'll be unforgettable. Those eyes!' For a moment she seemed about to confer some sort of embrace, then her husband entered the *salon* and the moment passed.

From the next morning forth, the Ayatollah Ruhollah Khomeini never appeared in public without his black burnoose and robe. He practised a fixed owl-like stare, and he noticed that his followers and counsellors were cowed by his fiery glance. He used to go over to Deanna's and practise a deliberate walk and some gestures she gave him. And then the lightning struck; the Shah was dethroned and the Ayatollah left Paris from one morning to the next, called to re-enter his kingdom.

'Well, I'm certainly sorry to hear about that,' said Miss Durbin when she learned of his departure. 'I was starting to get really fond of the old darling. I wonder what'll happen to him now.'

The hostage crisis happened to him and Jimmy Carter happened to him, or perhaps he happened to Jimmy Carter. The CIA did nip-ups in the desert and one or two minor Canadian diplomats fancied they'd put something over on him, and then came Reagan, the terrifying fall in oil prices, the near-dissolution of OPEC and the faithless, un-Islamic behaviour of the Iraqi and the need to make *jihad* upon them, the necessity of killing and killing, mining the Gulf, striking down the Great Beast, and his counsellors proliferated and he didn't want to be Clarabelle Cow and the clamour rose as he collapsed into senile impotence. Voices shrilled, hands caught at his sleeves, pushed him through rooms and now he thinks of the glorious ringing voice and the soft plump arms and knows that he is dying.

Jolene from Moline

BRONSON IS DOING WELL in middle age. Sure he's older but he's a big hit with everybody in the field and goes around giving *seminars*. He hasn't felt quite the same about himself since he had to give a neighbour at the lake the news that his father had died. Bronson doesn't care to be the bearer of bad news; this can get you into deep stew. Good news can too, so what are you going to do? Head for the storm cellar when the big winds start to circulate? Mind your own business? Don't get too attached to pets! Keep phone calls to Gary or Irene well under three minutes. Well, say ten minutes. He has to say something to Viv about this.

'Hey, I mean, hey look, Toronto, 925-0143. And again here, 925-0143. And here, Coral Gables. Coral Gables? Who do we know lives in Coral Gables?'

'The chief. That's one of your calls. You made that call on a weekend.'

'I can't have done. Thirty-seven dollars? That's ridiculous, I mean the Bell are out of their minds. I never made any thirty-seven-dollar phone calls.'

'Face it, Bronson! You've started making overseas calls. Your life is changing, you know that? You called London four times last month. Look on the bill, there it is, London, four times.'

'Those were under-one-minute messages. Two dollars. I rehearsed the conversation before I came on the line.'

'... and last week you told me you'd been using an on-line library catalogue. Three-by-five index cards aren't good enough for you any more, it's going to be all keyboarding from now on, Mr Bronson.'

'Who made seven calls to Stoverville?'

'Stoverville is a mythical place,' says Vivie piously.

This is not an argument either of them can win, what we call a no-win situation, one of those phrases birthed by the media and either meaningless or false: a no-win situation, state-of-the-art technology, information retrieval and storage, distinct society, baby on board, presidential irresponsibility, bloodbath.

Bloodbath was news for most of one summer. Bronson hasn't heard a word about bloodbath for ten weeks; it's a cold story. So are the contras, Imelda Marcos and her two thousand shoes, quadraphonic recording, Las Malvinas, Pia Zadora, Liz Taylor, Mick Jagger....

'Suppose we agree to leave the phone alone? Write a letter. A stamp costs less than long distance.'

'The post office was the creature of literacy,' says Vivie, 'and will perish with it.'

'My bottom line,' says Bronson, 'is that a stamp will cost more than a call to London on the day after I'm buried. It's more a twenty-first century thing. There was a time when there were no post offices, and there will be again, and just before that it will cost a million dollars to get a letter from here to Kansas. I'm losing my hold on life, do you realize that, Viv? There are too many things I don't care about any more. The World Series, I mean, who could care? The Emmy Awards. The Russians. Would you ever have believed that a time would come when we weren't scared of the Russians? Gorbachev will be on the Letterman show one of these nights. I don't care what the Russians do. Life's too short.'

'It isn't that short. It's really just getting started.'

But Viv has small folds and wrinkles just at the angle where her arms fit into their sockets beside the breasts. Little folds, just shadows, not even lines. 'Browning,' says Bronson.

'Why Browning?'

'Good advice for mauppies. Middle-aged urban professionals.'

'Are you telling me something with elaborate indirection?'

'I think I have to be there, sweetie.'

'Again?'

'"Fraid so.'

'Poor baby! What is it this time?'

'An experiment, it's just a controlled experiment. We've got these twenty-four fast-food users, convenience-food junkies. The problem is to see how long they can survive on the basic burger diet.'

'You're making this up!'

'Vivie, Vivie, *Vivie*, would I lie to you?'

'Well would you?'

'And we've got a control group of two dozen vegetarians and health-food nuts, all volunteers. They've signed waivers and they all get the same fee and up to forty-five hundred calories daily depending on their felt needs.'

'Go on, get out of here. Party animal!'

'No, really!'

'You and your sportive play of imagination. What you've got there are Puritans versus Sensualists and so far it's Sensualists-73, Puritans-0. A rout.'

'Don't be too sure. I think the Puritans are creeping up. I suspect they're a great second-half club, hard to hold a lead on. Anyway ...' (briskly, nonchalantly), 'I really do have to go. I'll be gone three days. It's all media folklore, you know, that's all it is. Take care of yourself, my darling, and leave that phone alone. I'll ring you from Kansas City.'

'I'll be sitting here waiting.'

Bronson doesn't really like these swings through the midwest any more than Viv likes having him out of her sight. In a town like Lincoln or Lawrence there isn't even any point to padding your expenses; there's nothing to spend the money on. It's the Holiday Inn or the Journey's End or the Travelodge and Bronson has reached that state of life in which luxury has no appeal for him. The paper wrappings on the water glasses and the plastic bottles of shampoo and the sample-sized bars of Zest are the same no matter where you stay. In Lawrence, Kansas, it's the Travelodge in an all-day rain, and a downed 707 at Kansas City International.

'Are you all right?' demands Viv when he calls her.

'Oh, sure, sure, but I thought I'd ring you. I saw the crater when the limo brought me out.'

'Crater?'

'Where the jet hit the hillside; there's very heavy fog tonight. It was still smoking.'

'Oh, my darling,' says Viv wildly, 'come back to me.'

'Now cut that out!'

'Have you seen Roger?'

'Tomorrow. I'll call you tomorrow night after my presentation.'

'I thought that was Thursday.'

Checks itinerary. 'You know, you're right. Tomorrow I'm in the seminar room at the food institute all day. Wow!'

'Sooner you than me.'

'I'm hanging up now, Viv. I'm putting the phone down. I'm hanging up now, bye-bye. Hang up, Viv!' He can hear the voice in the receiver until he breaks the connection. 'Goddamn woman!'

Then he looks at TSN for a while but they keep jumping from baseball to basketball to hockey to golf in bright true colour, the greens enchanting, the hockey-jerseys in bang-on bad taste, eventually Bronson is watching for the colour, paying no attention to the scores. The huge screen is exactly framed in the window-wall of his motel room; there is this swimming delightful composition in a full spectrum and wrapped around it is a powerful grey vista. Outside in the deepening dusk the wide lawns of the motel are soaking, and behind the building in a little hollow that declines from Bronson's window frame a smallish lake is starting to form. A hundred yards away the Interstate slices off the edge of town and ramps and access roads gleam with moving fog lights. He waits.

Roger calls about ten and instructs him to pick up dinner at HoJos, just across the parking lot. There's a protective canopy and he can make it to the restaurant without getting soaking wet.

'No sense in both of us drowning in it. I'm having trouble with my distributor and I can't guarantee an arrival time. They also have the all-day big-breakfast special which I can recommend, fits right in with our research, home fries, pancakes, choice of syrup – try the cinnamon flavoured. I'll have Jolene pick you up at, say, nine-fifteen, all righty?'

'Jolene?'

'One of my graduate students, very conscientious. You'll know her all right.'

'How?'

'She'll be wearing a conference name tag with the IYN logo, and it'll have her picture on it, sweet thing, Jolene Frager. She's got a cute little Honda. She'll drive you to the institute. First seminar at 10:05 in the green conference room. "Use of pre-packaged relishes and condiments in speeded-up takeout service: a symposium." You're one of the professional respondents. Maybe you'd better go over your notes tonight. At 11:15 we move to the red room to discuss control of excessive paper napkin use. Lunch at 1:00. Workshops in the afternoon. You're doing promo and public-relations. Anything you need, one of the girls can get it for you. If you don't see it, be sure to ask for it. Good night, old friend.'

'Good night, Roger.' Bronson expects to dream about the International Year of Nutrition, and the war between the health-food nuts and the fast-food junkies, but for some reason he dreams about an American bittern he once saw standing quietly and gazing at him out at his summer place. That bird had had very green legs.

He wakes up twice in the night to the sound of heavy rain. In the morning the lake is lapping at his window frame, not yet quite high enough to flood the room. The building has that look of impermanence that motel construction shares with the Ark. For a moment he thinks about sending forth a dove to see if it comes back, then decides to go over and have the big-breakfast special. Pancakes, he thinks, home fries. There is much – almost everything – to be said in defence of pancakes and home fries and a double order of bacon and syrup and juice and three cups of coffee, and quite as much to be said in defence of Ms Frager who, while not exactly fetching an olive twig to Mount Ararat, brings news that the flood trails no cyclones in its wake. No retreat to storm cellar impends.

'I listened to the weather 'cause I knew you'd want to hear,' she says in a soft clear voice. 'Highs of forty-two through forty-eight predicted, with a fifty percent chance of precipitation.'

61

Deep in his coffee mug, Bronson pays little heed, but wonders privately where they come from, the little groupeenas, the female hangers-on who run after ballplayers and other jocks, speakers at conferences, and poets. He remembers that this one has a cute little Honda; he stares at it as they cross the dripping parking lot.

'It's rusted raht out,' says Jolene, twitching the hood of her waterproof cape well up over her head and ears, 'but it'll take us round to the institute all raht. They's 150,000 miles on this car. I just use it to go home for weekends.'

They snake into mid-morning traffic on an Interstate access past the other seven motels, Burger King, Chicken Ranch, a pair of soaring golden arches and where the road rises upwards in front of them towards a high horizon shining in mist and grey light the logos of chains never seen at home. He has come to that mystical state where all burgers resolve themselves into the essential item of convenience food service and he makes a mental note to re-title his remarks for the afternoon workshop.

'That all hamburgers are One,' he says to himself, feeling like Plato. In the ancient controversy over whether takeout business is more desirable – closer to The Good – than your basic sit-down customer, he resolves to come down on the Platonic side, as he understands it. It's true that takeout service generates volume and reduces wear and tear on fixtures, especially washroom facilities, but long-term patronage can only be evolved from repeat sitdown adult visits. There is even something to be said for golden-age cards and senior citizens. Trying these ideas out on Jolene, he remarks that we cannot expose the aged on hillsides to starve.

'Oh, I just couldn't agree more, Mr Bronson,' she says adoringly. 'I think our old people have the same rahts as everybody and especially the raht to socialize with dignity. I think we should provide them with free morning newspapers and unlimited coffee refills. Well, maybe not unlimited, but up to three cups and that should hold them, the old darlings.' She swings the car into a reserved parking space and leads him up a stairway, through a pair of heavy service doors, and along a series of mazy corridors. They arrive at the friendly, wide-open doors of the green seminar raht – right – on time. Just inside are ranks of tables bearing sample packages of catsup, red and green relish, several flavours of vinegar, stiff paper salt and pepper containers in a variety of sizes and competing lines. In prominent display positions on the green walls are vast graphs detailing cost/consumption ratios. It is a state-of-the-art conference situation. Bronson feels pleasure at the impression of Jolene's soft dry cool palm in his as she leads him to the respondent's bucket seat. She leaves him with a lingering glance and goes to the coat racks where she wriggles out of her rainwear and sits modestly at the rear of the students' section. The conference takes off. Bronson finds himself in top form, witty, responsive, original, caring.

After ninety minutes of rapier-like give and take the opening session concludes. The questions have been good questions; the recurring conference participant who dismisses the whole undertaking as meaningless and irrelevant has not surfaced. They move over to the red room and Bronson finds himself starting to imagine lunch at the faculty club. He starts to salivate, feeling guilty because he isn't imagining burgers and fries. He's thinking of lightly grilled lake trout followed by something in a béarnaise sauce; the faculty club here has three-star status, *nouvelle cuisine*, but superb. He rises to answer an inquiry about pop-up napkin dispensers, quoting impressive statistics on shipment of cartons of two dozen packages of two hundred to the trade, and after comes the eating of the steaks, the luncheon badinage. Jolene is nowhere to be seen.

'Ms Frager?' says Roger absently. 'I gave her an assignment for part of the afternoon. Heller to research, that one.'

All the same, late in the afternoon of the first day, Bronson heard a door slide open on insecure tracks and saw a shaft of sunlight glittering with dust motes as it lanced into the workshop from across the neighbouring corridor. He thought he glimpsed the figure of Jolene framed in the late sun but he wasn't certain. The door slid shut, greyness descended again as he continued his remarks. 'Marketing is the overall form of life under which promotion and PR may be subsumed as modes. Everything fits into marketing somewhere. Think of the Gospel, if you remember the Gospel. The word means "the good news" and marketing men are bringers of the good news. In this sense, perhaps only in this sense, every product is holy, sacred. It doesn't matter what it is; it exists and it has its own being. The marketing man is never ashamed of himself, never feels brash or unwelcome. He does what he has to do because his deepest responsibility is to his product, and the product is his deepest expression of himself. Now take your basic franchise situation....'

Here his voice wandered away with his thoughts. The young person who had just come in was sitting hunched well forward eyeing him, hanging on his words, certainly his little groupeena of the morning. He traced out her form in the shadows of the back row, feeling a pang as he realized how slight she was, how slender and young.

'Glinda,' he thought, 'the good bitch, the good little bitch.'

'When you cross the river into Saint Louis,' he said, 'now you've all been there and you know what I'm going to say. When you cross the river the first thing you see is....'

'The arch,' they shouted with a single voice.

'Raht on! Gateway to the West. But the thing is, marketing men were using the golden arches before there was an arch leading to Saint Louis. They'd chosen that symbol first, and the promoters in Saint Louis were following in their steps. If you select a symbol, a logo, with genuine inspiration, the generations will follow you.'

'Like the Cross,' said a voice.

'Or the swastika,' said Bronson. 'They had it in India first and it moved mountains.'

'Can't do without the logos,' said a male student.

'In the beginning was the logo,' said Bronson cheerfully; detaching himself from the mob. He wished he had a drive back to the Travelodge. He had four or five hours ahead of him of careful editing of the Thursday night presentation. *Meeting pure-food standards in franchised operations.* The chief had given him the task with many compliments on his verbal skills which seemed to Bronson to mask a heavy threat. Who can drink, he thought to himself, of the cup that I drink, the bottomless mug of endless refills? Interest groups might oppose him, yet franchised food service had swept civilization as we have known it. The quarter-pounder had conquered where Marx, Darwin, Nietzsche, Freud, Heidegger had withered to dust. What's the good word, he thought, playing with his pencil. He made many revisions to his text, tightening and adjusting, shivering in his draughty room as a low-pressure system moved out of the area and cold clear air swept down from the great plains. He slept uneasily, only taking a light breakfast when he awoke; there would be a formal dinner before his presentation, a faculty party afterwards, and here, swinging her keys, came Jolene to deliver him to the morning workshop. She sat down across from him and he offered her a sausage which she gently rejected. But there was no acridity in the rejection. Bronson encouraged her to talk about herself.

'I was so pleased when you spoke about the Gateway to the West yesterday. I've seen the arch many times on my way down river. I used to take 67 south from Moline to East Saint Louis and then get onto 3 right into Carbondale where my boyfriend Bubba is a lab demonstrator.'

Bronson felt irritation at this talk of boyfriends. This serviceable woman had no business to have a boyfriend Bubba in Carbondale.

'Anymore I just come across on Interstate 80 to Des Moines and down 35 to K C and on out here.'

'Moline,' said Bronson, fumbling for truth. 'Does that make you Jolene from Moline?'

'Sure enough does,' she said, lowering her eyes. She had faced this before.

'That's so ... so musical,' said Bronson. He felt a wave of good cheer overwhelm him. 'Are you coming to the morning workshop?'

'I'm your wheels,' she said, 'but I've got my experiments to supervise. I'll be there tonight though. I wouldn't miss it for anythang.' Bronson noticed that she wore a primrose-coloured blouse with tiny red and blue flowers embroidered on the open collar near the hollow of her throat. Her jeans were the blue of a summer sky. He cleared his throat nervously. 'Do you ever develop promo material on your own?'

'Oh, but I surely do, why all the time. It's how I want to help defend a great industry. I feel that franchise food is more important even than rock and roll.'

This judgement thrilled Bronson's blood. He made a point of working it into his evening presentation. It seemed to him that they were all overcrowded into a big lecture auditorium; there must have been 325 people there, including a sampling of the subjects in the fast food/health nut experiment. The Dean of the Communications programme was there and leading nutritionists, and a good half of the conference members. He gave a great reading; they laughed in all the right places, the health-food nuts blushed and stood abashed. Jolene admired him from the last row. He received a rising ovation when he showed his two videos. At the end he was hemmed in by dignitaries but all he wanted to do was pick up a ride to Roger's for the party where, he knew, he would be petted and made much of. It would all be worth it, the requests for statements, the cassette tapings of his least utterances, the very strong highballs which he would have to keep leaving on bookshelves because Jolene was there and she wanted to talk to him about her writing. This must have been a familiar behaviour pattern for everybody there; they were instantly left alone on a davenport. A line from somewhere came into poor Bronson's head. 'She's only here for you to fuck.' He listened to Jolene with grave courtesy, putting her manuscripts into his file folder; he kissed her hand. She was still wearing the primrose blouse with the delicate flowers. Just a magnificent woman. 'Take down my address,' he urged, 'for if I can help you in any way you only have to try to reach me. Be sure to call ahead now!' She promised that she would, left the party and got into her rusted-out Honda, and drove away and he hasn't heard from her yet.

He can see her in hallucinatory detail, the tender wisps of hair at her temples, the blondness, the eager posture, the sweet throat. On the way home Bronson knows that he isn't in Kansas any more but he hopes someday to go back.

NOTE TO THE READER: This story has profited from the editorial awareness of John Metcalf, who advised the author that 'scrumpy,' far from being a weak fizzy near-cider suitable for ladies, is a most potent brew often known to cause large men the sudden loss of the use of their legs.

The word 'tales' is used in the title in view of John Metcalf's well-known aversion to employment of this term in literary discourse. HH.

Two Bridport Tales

GO LOOKING FOR AN ANCESTOR, a family, and you will only find a genealogy, headstones, rank grass: look for a house with a woman inside it and you may walk into a new life, a world, a way of responding to intricate systems of acting. Bridport, like any town, was a collection of ways to feel, converse, to transact affairs, a puzzle to which I had no clue. Until I located a respondent I had no means of entry to the maze and, once in, no way of returning to my starting place. When, therefore, I succeeded in identifying a particular house in a long terrace, 'a Grade Two listed dwelling,' as *our* house, I knew that I must soon find the trace of a connection. I haunted the museum, I examined old title deeds and wills, I surveyed the ground. I made my preparations.

At last I knocked on the door of the house in South Street and was instantly admitted by Mistress Minnie Dunford, eighty-one, brave, purblind, blue with damp cold. Only one bar of the electric fire was lighted on this foggy morning; the parlour reeked of spongy wood and upholstery, maybe of wet rot. There was a vast profusion of photographs and knick-knacks displayed on every wall and shelf, which I scrutinized covertly while the old Dorset woman bustled about the room, picking up china objects and putting them down, presents from Weymouth and Puddletown and Beaminster. She showed me pictures of hedgers and furze-cutters and mowers and thatchers, crafts which might have been supposed to be banished from the earth at the end of the last century but which were preserved in all their complex splendour in Minnie Dunford's eyes.

'My father worked in Gundry rope-walk,' she crooned, as though beginning a well-beloved old song, 'up behind the houses and shops along of West Street. And later he were out to Pymore Mills, but he went to the first German war, you see, and were never satisfied after that, couldn't settle down like. He were a restless man.'

She took a photograph of her father from the chimneypiece and showed it to me pridefully.

'So he was a sergeant,' I said.

'He were that, sir, in the county regiment as has its headquarters in Dorchester as you come in along the Bridport road. These were his medals, all four as you can see.'

The group of four medals, mounted as worn, comprised a World War I trio and, which rather surprised me, a Distinguished Conduct Medal named to 10573 Sgt. R.H. Bodmer, 2nd Batt., the Dorset Reg't. The medals were in mint condition, their original ribbons faded but uncreased.

I commented on the gallantry award.

'Aye, that were when he hurt himself on the wire, barbed wire that were, in some great attack, but I couldn't tell you the date or time of it. I have all his documents, which you might examine if you liked, sir.'

She took down from their customary resting place a number of other curios and mementoes, framed photographs of sailors, gilt candlesticks, silk handkerchiefs from China. I noticed that she was wearing three thick woollen jumpers, one over the next, and yet gave no impression of bulk. I thought she must be a thin little woman. I spotted a fine pair of Chelsea dogs which she took up one after the other, handled with jealous care, exhibited briefly, then returned to their place. I decided that it might be time to prosecute my own inquiries, and made an appropriate overture. 'This house once belonged to my family,' I said, producing my own collection of snapshots, gleaned from museum research. 'Here is a picture of somebody who may have been a third cousin once removed. He lived here in the nineteen-thirties.' I handed over the photograph.

'Why, to be sure, 'tis old Cracky. And there's William. This must be William's wedding, sir. This was the grocer's, you see. This house and the next, 'twas all one. They do be standing in the garden. Here, come and see.'

She led me through the rearwards parts of the dwelling to the plot of ground outside where some antiquated trelliswork stood up covered with vines and mosses. There was a paralysing damp sweat

on the ground. I shivered as she examined the photograph labori-
ously. It was clear that she could only just make it out.

'Like a great-uncle, ye say?'

'Not quite as close as that. He descends from my great-great-
great-great-grandfather. We have the same family name.'

'Arthur,' she said, quite correctly, 'he were an Arthur, and young
William – this is his wedding-day – were John William. He lived
over the shop until the last war and died in Africa, they say. He
were a brewer's boy; he worked just down the road and when he
died the brewery took the house to complete a parcel of land. I only
as rents from them. You might pay a call on them, sir. My man
rented from the brewers when they divided the house, and I kept
the place on after he were gone though it do be far too much for me
at my time of life. Buried him from here, I did, matter o' ten years
ago, in the churchyard of Saint Mary's.' She began to smile grimly,
and led me back to the best front room where the electric fire could
now scarcely be seen in a gathering mist.

'Laid him out among our belongings, just here.' She made a
sweeping gesture with her arms. ''Twas before we boarded up the
hearth. We'd a great fire to drive out the damp; we made all snug for
him. The waggoners crafted the box, everything tidy like, and they
had him on a pair of little trestles as stood just here ... and here.
And the flowers, you never saw such flowers. And after we put him
to rest they all came back with me and the lad, and we gave them
their drinks. There were port for the rector, such glasses as he
drank. He were a good-living easy man. Perhaps you've spoken to
him, sir, before he parted from us?'

'Canon Ewings, wasn't it?'

'That were he, sir. Thirty year and more he were among us.
Very highly connected was Canon Ewings and a man of great kindness. He would perform his little offices, the baptizing, marrying,
burying, very gentlemanlike. He liked his glass of port, did he, and
for the others mostly we had the ale from over the way at the
brewer's yard, which they sent as a gift, the best ale. Taylor's
Magnificent Old Dorset Ale. Some o' the gentlemen, they took
their scrumpy.'

She pronounced it 'scrooompy' with a very long vowel. Scrumpy appears to be some cider-like beverage innocent enough in its approach to you, but known often to cause large men the sudden loss of the use of their legs. Much enjoyed at funerals.

'Canon Ewings were your great clergyman for obsequies. He would officiate with all his canonicals about him; never the smallest omission of what might be due and proper. He spoke over my Edward for most an hour, what a good man he were, and how the old ways were ending when men like my Edward disappeared from the streets of Bridport. He were a carter for Taylor's and he drove a team of four and sometimes six horses with a great load of casks all around about, to Burton Bradstock, up the cliff road to the golf-house. Afterwards when they put the horses down he drove a lorry, forty year and more first to last. A familiar figure, 'twas what Canon said, a familiar figure on the streets of this town, and never an accident nor a drop spilled nor man nor woman put in danger by his beasts.'

Her eyes kept straying towards the pair of Chelsea dogs as though she were uncertain of their presence. I commented on them to reassure her. 'Your Chelsea ware must be the admiration of all your friends, such a fine clear glaze and an undamaged pair, quite like new.'

'Why, sir,' she chuckled, "twas exactly what poor Canon Ewings said to me.'

'After the funeral?'

'Aye.'

'Was he a collector then?'

'He were a collector, sir, at all times and opportunities. Known for his acquisitive ways, he were. Mind, it were the custom, as you must know, to offer Rector a present for his own use 'stead of a sum of money, for he would never take money from poor folk. Very admired he were for those kind intentions. He would come back after the burial and stand among the mourners, casting his eyes over the room, or would ask to be shown through the upper rooms, as a politeness like. Often there would be some little old piece, a chair as might be, or a piece of needlework worked long ago, candlesticks, pewter or silver, a warming pan against the damp, or little tables. You could always tell when Rector had his eye special on some requital of his grace. Very partial to paste. Paste settings of the last century. He were known for that. And chairs. I often helped a friend to carry a pair of chairs to the rectory.'

'He must have been a great collector.'

'I believe as you could say so truly, sir. When the afflicted saw how the land lay, when they saw the light in Rector's eyes at some bit of lacquer – for he never asked for anything and would never take more than a single object, or at most a pair, size no consideration, they were expected to offer it in thanks. Rectory were fair bursting, sir, with little tables, inlaid and fancy turned or with pineapples. Aye and sometimes big tables, settles, spindled cabinets. He were fond of a dark grain of wood.'

'And he had his eye on your Chelsea dogs?'

'Well-beloved they were, both by me and by my Edward. They're very old and very good. I know that for I saw Canon's eyes gleam when he spied them. "Oh, my," said he, "Mistress Dunford. Oh, be truly joyful." My husband just in the ground. "Be joyful that you have the pair, for without the pair you can expect nothing. Must have both." It was a-tremble on my lips to offer them to him, but something stayed my voice, and I cast around for another offering like. I went into the kitchen and came back with a present from Lowestoft, a pretty little blue saucer with a vessel on it breasting the seas and I put it into his hands. He were full of admirings but at the same time disappointed. I couldn't give him my dogs, could I, sir?'

'For certain you could not, Mistress Dunford.'

'I'm afraid that I erred by vainglory, for I felt the humorous side of it, and I said, "Canon, I do beg your pardon but I wonder if you could tell me what such a fine pair of animals would fetch if I were to sell them?" I saw the gleam in his eyes again. "I might offer forty pounds for the pair," he said and I almost fainted dead away, for they came from my Edward's family and I never knew they were so precious. Forty pounds! I thought to ask for the forty pounds on the instant, but I noticed that the Rector's eyes had grown very small and sharp and I said to myself that if he would give forty there might be others as would give more.'

'Others would have given a hundred at that time,' I said, 'and today much more.'

'I thought so, the cunning old fellow. But there, I oughtn't to speak harsh for he made no complaint, did Rector, knowing I had a proper notion of the little dogs' value. Aren't they the silly creatures though, with their simple faces and their shine?'

She went to the chimneypiece and stroked the neck of the right-hand piece as though it were a living creature. There was love in her touch.

'Then poor Canon was translated, you see, to a distant living. In Sussex they do say. It were not because of his disappointment over the little dogs, I'll do him that credit. Never reproached me by a look or a deed and were always friendly. He took away his bit of Lowestoft quick enough. But in the end he was taken from us while still in a green old age. To Sussex.'

She spoke of Sussex as though it were at the ends of the earth. I asked how long Canon Ewings had been gone, for I'd observed that his name had been painted over on the smart blue-and-gold notice board near the porch.

'Matter of two or three years, 'twould be. And it took three great lorries, pantechnicons they were, three of them, to empty the rectory of his belongings. You never saw such a deal of joinery, and all fine work, and draperies, and all sorts of lumber, paintings, and some no more than moderately decent. Glass. Three vans full; there were stories in the *Evening Echo* about our good rector's departure. A great collector is just what they said of him, but he didn't collect up my dogs, and there they sit, neat as ever.'

'And you heard no more about the great collector?'

'Ah, but we did, sir, and there's the sad jest of it. It were maybe six months ago, no more, that we heard of Canon Ewings again in the newspaper. He'd a new church, Saint Lucy's if I remember, in one of they lonely hill villages near the sea, Folkington under Long Man. That was it, Saint Lucy's, Folkington, and as folk tell me, near the pleasure resort of Eastbourne.'

I could readily picture the sedate and comfortable rector in semi-retirement, with little ecclesiastical duty to perform, running down into Eastbourne of an afternoon to take tea with a lady acquaintance.

'Aye, sir, that was the way of it, the poor man, with little enough to occupy his hours but his fine possessions. But then comes the terrible end of it all, for one afternoon while Canon Ewings was in Eastbourne, three great vans drew up to his rectory on the hill and looted it. They took away all his tables and chairs and fine things, leaving behind nothing at all except his poor cook tied up to a post in the cellarage where she might cry out for hours and never be heard. All of it gone.'

I thought I remembered something about the burglary in one of the London newspapers, perhaps the *Telegraph*. 'None of it ever recovered, I believe.'

'None of it, sir, from that day forward, and the whole of it valued at between forty and fifty thousand pounds.'

I must have shown some astonishment at the amount.

'That were the total all the same, sir, though you'd scarce believe it, and all picked up at Bridport marriages or funerals over the years. Forty thousand pounds!' She gave me a sly look and her face took on the appearance of a rosily withered apple. 'The collector collected, as you might say.' She laughed softly.

I wasn't sure just how to take this, the story lay so wryly on the tongue as to make one's mouth pucker. I may have shivered momentarily, moved by the peculiar impulse that makes one feel that heavy footsteps are traversing one's grave. Mistress Dunford stooped and moved the switch on the electric fire; presently a second orange bar began to gleam weakly in the obscure light. Naturally I thought of Thomas Hardy, whose name, fame, cast of mind, cover the countryside between Lyme and Weymouth like the most ironic of garments, the fine linen of burial. Hardy was full of similar jokes upon the comfortable, and as all the living are comfortable so far forward as they do not lie in damp earth, Hardy's joke was on everybody here.

I wondered about the local climate. Bridport lies inland a matter

YOU'LL CATCH YOUR DEATH

YOU'LL CATCH YOUR DEATH

of a mile or two from the Channel, on that enormous bight which some call West Bay and some call Dead Man's Bay. An unhandy sailing vessel and an unwary skipper might easily so position themselves in Dead Man's Bay as to be unable to sail out of it no matter how desperately the vessel might tack, the skipper pray for an offshore breeze. The cliffs are too high, the bight too broad, for a ship without machinery to sail out unaided. There remains nothing but the lee shore of Chesil Bank, grinding under the keel of coarse gravel, inrush of water in the bewildering mist. Bridport spins hemp and makes rope, twine, net, and sends them forth from Dead Man's Bay. Hardy's poem writes itself in the occupation and the names, but Hardy wrote little about the place. He may have judged the prevailing ironies of climate, situation, manufacture, too bald, too obvious, for poetical service, at the same time fanciful, unprosaic, ill-adapted material for fiction. This would have been an uncharacteristic decision on the part of the great novelist, whose art accepts the most brutal, most prosaic of accidents. I wondered whether the Hardyesque was born out of the grimness of the place – whether Hardy simply looked over the district and discovered himself – or whether the wry tone of Bridport anecdote derived from unconscious imitation of the supreme artist by the folk who lived under his eye. We often meet persons who live their lives, as they imagine, according to Shakespearian or Dickensian style. Hardy too may supply his native region with its manners and sense of humour. More than imaginary and evanescent Wessex, Hardy may have created Bridport, Beaminster, Dorchester, Weymouth, as they are, never mind his fictitious disguises for them, Port Bredy, Casterbridge. Here we arrive at the edges of counterpoised realities.

I stood there fumbling at these suspicions, shivering lightly, silent, none too clear-sighted in the misleading light of the parlour. Mistress Dunford, a generation older, not so strong, less able to withstand chill, frail, stood the bitter air better than I. She offered tea; there was an interval while the restoring drink was in preparation. I offered to step over the road for tinned biscuits but was refused. She could provide biscuits in profusion; the town was famous for its biscuits. I may just have mentioned the indwelling sense of the Hardyesque which the place communicated, and her face grew animated. She pushed the plate of excellent, extremely rich, almond-flavoured biscuits close to me, poured out the tea and made many appreciative exclamations. 'I were a maid when first I read his poems,' she said, 'but I remember them as though they were new. I remember one about a young wife who is making arrangements for her mourning clothes, all in the last new fashion, and her poor man finds her in the draper's shop while he coughs and coughs behind his chilly hand.'

'I know that one,' I said, 'and it always makes me fearful.'

'Life is fearful,' she said, 'and full of surprises for comfortable folk like my nephew Mr Vye, the undertaker.'

'Undertaker,' I quavered. The frail woman was beginning to have the aspect of one of the Norns, the northern Fates, spinners of our destinies. She pushed the plate of toothsome biscuits further towards my side of the tea-table, and poured out more of her scalding brew.

'Very given to cremations,' she said, eyeing the steam as it rose from the teapot, 'and couldn't bear Bridport for its wetness, he used to say. He would drive a hundred miles to fetch a body back to his furnaces in West Street. Mighty elaborate and odd were those furnaces, with wide flues and artistic brickwork. That were my sister's boy, but he never had the aspect of a boy. Grave-visaged and sombre and mighty well-suited to his trade. He began life as a joiner and progressed from that to coffin-maker. In the end he had little use for coffins, being more inclined to the crematorium. He were a specialist, and advertised as such.'

'It's a particular calling,' I said, 'not suited to everyone.'

'You say truth, sir. My nephew Edwin Vye would respond to any call for his services. I remember many times when he drove his hearse a matter of hundreds of miles to claim a body and bring it home for his crematorium. He would drive direct across country, leaving London on his right hand, and claim shipments at Heathrow airfield, if you can believe that. Right in under the noses of the great aeroplanes he would drive with his shiny hearse, to have the bodies tipped down the ramp for his claiming. Citizens of this town who had wandered abroad, idle silly folk, and died in foreign places of dangerous diseases. Which they would not have met with in Bridport, as I believe.'

Her tone took on an unmistakable asperity, mixed with much kindness and good sense. 'I lay it to his great fear of the damp. But in the end he had to give up his scamperings across country after corpses because of the arthritis. Crippling it were. He were more bent and twisted at sixty than I am at my age. Doctors recommended change of scene and warm climates, and poor Edwin was always much ordered about by his wife, who was eager to embark on one of them round-the-world-retirement cruises.'

I had a dreadful sense of the story's inner necessity and listened with paralysed attention while my tea grew cold and fragments of biscuits crumbled wetly in the saucer.

''Twas somewhere in the South Atlantic, the loneliest seas in the world and the most distant from anywhere, that poor Edwin met his end. Heart failure brought on by rheumatoid arthritis and hypertension, so that he never arrived in any warm southern place. The steamer was thousands of miles from the nearest land and the ship had no proper system of refrigeration, and the small number of passengers were none too ready to continue their holiday voyage with Edwin making one of the company. His poor wife protested, as she stated, but there were danger of contamination and grumbling from the holiday-makers so he were buried at sea, shot down a chute like one of his own arrivals at the airfield, though never to reach the comfort of his furnace.'

That was all Mistress Dunford had to say on the subject, leaving me with an ineluctable impression of fated pursuit; the lover of fire, the enthusiastic cremator, washed forever in the frigid sea.

Rig Flip

SO THERE we were bowling along in the right lane eastbound on 401, heading for Montréal and home about ten-thirty in the morning. It was a Tuesday or a Wednesday, I'm not too clear about that. Fran says it was Tuesday and I guess she's right, but I'm not too clear. We were coming back from opening up the cottage for the summer. I was driving. I treat a car right. I might have been doing seventy. That's 120 km. I understand kilometres all right. I know how to change them back and forth. Nobody was passing us and we weren't passing anybody, just cruising easy at 120 km. Good visibility. I check these things. I drove truck for thirty years.

We were on a flat stretch somewhere along past Brinston Road there. I remember seeing the overpass. I've got the signs on that stretch of highway pretty near memorized. Shanly Road exit, Brinston Road, Flagg Road – used to be Flegg Road – Hoasic Creek. The eastbound lanes are flat, with fairly thick brush off to your right, and a little further down there's one of those small, round houses, poured concrete, with a single door and window looking towards the highway. What are those buildings anyway? One of these days I'll stop for a piss and go over and sneak a peek in the window. Or maybe I won't, because it was just about there that it happened.

On the other side of the median the fields are clear and open. The ground rises slowly to the next ridge, maybe a mile – two kilometres maybe – to the east. There wasn't a single vehicle along the whole visible stretch, until a big rig came over the rise and started down in our direction, doing the maximum permitted, dead on a hundred in the slow lane. He looked great in the sun, a big new Western Star tractor painted pure shining white, looking like a windjammer in the clear morning light. Twenty-four-wheeler with the spares retracted, Fruehauf box without a mark on her. I didn't see the company identification. Might have been a rig out on leasing the way they all are nowadays. Companies don't figure to tie up

79

capital operating a fleet; they lease from a private operator for a set term. They might put the company logo on the box if it's a longish term, say three years. It might have been a private operation, I never did find out. He had a ton of paint on her. As we closed on each other I began to spot the painted trim, all red and gold and blue like flames, and above the grille, between a pair of scrolls or angel's wings it said, 'Pretty Linda'.

I can still see a long way at that.

Away off at the top of the rise to the east, almost invisible in the blended sun and shadow along the skyline, this little insect comes out of nowheres going like hell. 160 km. What's that? Sixty for the hundred, and divide the other sixty by five, twelve, and multiply by three, thirty-six, gives you ninety-six miles an hour. Stayed in the passing lane the whole time till it happened, overtaking the rig at the rate of more than sixty km. Rolling up alongside as if the overtaken vehicle was standing still. Gives you an idea, eh? Wasn't a Fiero. Wasn't an American car at all. Black and green in a phony Formula One configuration. Probably Japanese.

Swooped down the long slope out of the sun like a fighter plane on the attack. I don't know that the trucker ever saw the son-of-a-gun in his mirrors. He just came out of the sunlight, never slowed, never put his blinkers on, never nothing, didn't hang in the blind spot, just barrelled on past like the semi was parked somewhere.

Afterwards everybody kept asking me about the car. Who was driving? What colour was it, did I get the number, was it somebody from Québec? Well, it wasn't somebody from Québec because there was a number plate at the front. I recall that clear enough. We don't have a front number plate in Québec. Could have been a souvenir plate; that's true enough. There wasn't time to read it off anyway. They were about a hundred yards away from us and closing fast when it happened. The overtaking car went past the tractor at 160 km and *accelerating*. Who knows why?

And then for some unknown reason cut right in front of the truckdriver. I mean shaved his front wheels. Really cut him off. I couldn't believe it. They hadn't been out of the passing lane for the whole time I had them in sight, just hung there steady as a rock, and then to go and do that! My head snapped around to the left and I got a look at them as they went by to the west. Given the speed of their vehicle and mine, we passed at over 280 km, or around 175 miles an hour, and that's rapid motion. So I only caught a glimpse of the interior of the driving compartment and I couldn't swear to anything. Police kept after me, you know. Did I see who was driving? I never said it to them because I didn't want to go around making accusations, but I think it was a woman that was driving. That's only my impression; they weren't quite abreast of me when she cut in; they were just coming up to me. I just caught them out of the corner of my eye as they went past and disappeared out of the story. They might not have realized what happened, the speed they were going. They weren't the kind to keep checking their mirrors.

Frances and me, we're still moving, you see, heading east at freeway speed, so I can't judge. I couldn't say. And right then I turned my head back to look at the tractor, and damned if everything didn't slow down. The picture. What I was seeing. I never would have believed it. Everything went rubbery and slowed down, and then froze. The driver cut sharply to his right when the other fellow shaved him. But he didn't brake, and that left him with nowhere to go but the right shoulder. He gets out on the gravel very quick and starts to lose the feel of the surface, you see, starts to skate, so he turns back, still pulling with all the tractor's power. Never geared down, just kept pulling. I guess he figured he still had full control of the box, but he was really sliding off half sideways, and the shoulder was only a lane and a half wide there, going down on the far right into the drainage and the fences and the fields, and then it happened.

It wasn't like television at all. It was like kind of x-ray eyes or something. You could see exactly what was happening inside the box. I mean, here was this big white shiny surface, not a mark on her, and suddenly she all starts to shiver. It was almost like you could see little wiggly lines along the side, kind of a visible vibration. Franny said, 'My God, George,' in a quiet little voice. She never saw anything like that before, even when she used to ride with me. You could judge how the whole load shifted as the tractor swung her round and the shoulder crumbled under the right wheels. You could guess from seeing it that it was a bulk load. We found out later that it was tonnes of bagged sugar in hundred-pound sacks (fifty kilos?) that they hadn't loaded carefully enough. When the box came round whole rows of them collapsed to one side. A couple of tonnes of sacked sugar. Then the whole darn load fell off to the right of the box and over she goes.

By the time I got us stopped and pulled well over off the driving lane, we were a couple of hundred yards off. I jumped out of the car and ran across the eastbound lanes and onto the median strip without even looking to see what was coming. I heard Fran holler at me, 'Watch where you're going, idiot!' I knew she'd come after me. The median drops down to a culvert and a drain just there. I found myself running in a ditch. I was watching for smoke and as I climbed out the other side of this ditch I looked to see if there were any signs of trouble, but all there was was a lot of creaking and breaking noises, as though the insides of the box were coming apart.

When I got up beside the wreck I heard other noises, a metallic grinding noise like you might hear in a machine shop, the sound of metal tearing. And there were cracking, splitting sounds, and a rushing sound like liquid pouring out of a drum. This all happened in a distorted way. I heard each sound separately, not blended together the way they would normally be if you heard them casually, just passing down the street. I stood back for a moment and wondered what that liquid was. I looked the whole length of the westbound lanes from the top of the ridge in the east to the Brinston Road overpass in the west. There wasn't a single vehicle in sight in either direction. Talk about your population explosion! No help in sight for miles.

Only one thing to do. The tractor was heeled over on its side at a better than ninety-degree angle, left front and rear wheels up in the air, still turning very slowly, which surprised me. Must have been freshly lubricated. The way the driver's compartment was angled over towards the drainage ditch it would be hard to climb out of, even if you weren't injured. I had to climb up onto the upper side of the cab by the left door to see if I could haul the driver out or help

him climb up or whatever. I had trouble with the climb. I had to
find a foothold but all the fittings on the tractor were out of their
normal position. The doors and the footrests and the wheels were
all up in the air and out of reach. I went back between the tractor
and the box and looked at the coupling and right there I saw the
source of the tearing and grinding noises. When she went over the
metal coupler had been wrenched and torn all out of shape. There
were ends of steel like knives sticking up, right where I had to put
my foot to give myself a boost. I got by them without stabbing
myself, hauling myself up by the cross-member of the tractor chas-
sis and the housing for the springs till I could work my way along
beside the sleeping compartment. Then I stood up on the side of
the tractor and eased my way along towards the door. I felt like I was
standing on a parapet, really high up off the ground.

When I got up beside the door I was relieved to find that the
window was open. I wouldn't have been able to get the door open. It
was shut solid, twisted and sprung out of line when the cab rolled.
It would likely have to be cut open with a torch when they got the
vehicle into the shop. I hoped the rig was fully insured.

I thought I saw another transport coming our way from the west,
just emerging from the overpass. I reckoned I'd have help in a minute. I stuck my head down through the open window and there he
was, right down at the bottom of the cab in what would ordinarily
be the passenger's position, slumped onto the right-side doorway,
out colder than a flounder. Nothing for it but to go in and get him
out before she blew.

I held back for a second or two. The truck was coming up fast in
the eastbound lane. I thought for sure he'd start braking to a stop
just across the median. Franny was standing down in the middle of
the median ditch, getting her feet soaking wet and waving to the
passing rig, and you know what? He never even slowed up. Went
right on by. He might have thought I was the driver, just getting out
of the cab. He might have alerted the OPP on CB. I'll give him the
benefit of the doubt. One of those big Ontario-Maritime rigs, I
believe it was, or maybe GTL. I can't be sure. They make the drivers
work to very tight schedules and very long hours. Perhaps he'd been

driving all night and was eager to clock in at his destination. He never paid any attention to us.

I had to go down in and I was starting to smell the gas leaking from a fractured tank. I didn't like it one bit. We carry a little extinguisher in our trunk but it wouldn't be a damn bit of good on a thing this size, and it looked to me that Fran had forgotten all about it in the excitement. I tried to get her to look up at me but she was staring at the truck that had gone past us, and if I know her she was repeating all the dirty words she knows, and she knows a few including some I never taught her. I had to get down inside, so I hitched around on my rear end and lowered my legs into the cab, feeling around for a bit of support, only there was nothing. It was like climbing down inside a mine shaft. There was some light through the windshield but none from the windows in the doors. I wasn't sure I'd ever get out. Finally I had to let myself fall on top of him; nothing else I could do. He never let out a peep. I thought he might be dead from a skull fracture or a broken neck. He felt warm though. Not a sound out of him as I felt around looking to get a grip on him. He was wearing a cheap sleeveless shirt, polyester and cotton, which might not hold at all if I tried to lift him with it. I craned my head back and looked up at the open window of the left-side door, which now formed a kind of skylight right above us. I couldn't tell you the exact dimensions because the cab was tilted so far off line. I was on my knees beside the driver, all jammed in next to the glove compartment with him half beside me and half under my knees. There was no room at all and even if I'd been able to stand up the window would have been a couple of feet over my head. I could just about reach it if I stretched my arms up but it would be a tough spot to get out of even if I only had myself to lift. And I had the driver to cope with and he was right out of it. I suddenly thought to check, and by golly the ignition was still switched on! What a jerk I am. I should have looked first thing. I reached up along the dashboard and turned it off but I couldn't get the key out of the lock; maybe there was some anti-theft device that retained them. They wouldn't slide out of the lock and I had no time to waste over them.

I worked him around and around till I got his head and shoulders and trunk upright with the rest of him sitting on the downside door which was flat on the sloping ground. Then I braced my legs and feet under me and got my arms around his waist. I tried to get his arms swung round over my shoulders with his head on my neck. No way I could work him into a fireman's lift, no room to move. When I thought I had hold of him securely, with the weight of his upper body lying on mine, I tried to extend my arms and legs and slide him upwards along the seat-back towards the window overhead. Boy, it was cramped in there. In about ten seconds I was sweating as hard as I've ever sweated in my life. He was a moderate-sized man, might have weighed about 170, but he was floppy.

If you've ever lifted a side of beef you'll know what I'm talking about. There's a kind of hinge along the join of the leg and trunk which folds and flops around when you try to hoist it; it's a very unhandy weight, and a human torso is exactly the same, hard to get a grip on.

He seemed much heavier than a carton or a crate of the same weight would be, and much harder to lift. He seemed to be pressing down on me like dead weight. I suddenly smelled a very strong sweetish smell like syrup or fresh baked goods, mixed with the smell of his sweat and a very sharp smell of running gasoline. I dream of those three smells some nights.

I struggled to straighten my legs and force him upwards towards the window, steadying him against the seat back. I thought we were getting somewhere when all at once he rolled away from me and I lost sight of his upper torso. I thought the wreck had shifted but actually he'd rolled into the sleeping bunk. I'd been shoving in the wrong direction.

I heard Frances calling to me, scolding. 'George? Georgie! You come out of there this instant, do you hear me?' Maybe she thought I was trying to act like some big hero, but if she'd been in there beside me she'd have known what was what. I'm no hero. I started thinking about getting out of there. I could have managed to escape by myself but there he was. I still don't know his name. He certainly didn't do anything to help; he just lay there. What are you going to do?

'Hang on, George, they're coming.'

You're a real bundle of good news, Franny. Who's coming? What are they going to do? I was still wrestling with my unconscious buddy and I was starting to realize that I couldn't do it. I just wasn't strong enough to lift him up and hike him through that skylight. I could have done it years ago but not any more. The muscles in my arms were fluttering and my legs had lost their power. I hadn't managed my energy very smartly. Damned sugar stank like it was melting into syrup. I struggled to get out of my jacket. I should have taken it off first thing. And the gas. Oh, God, I was so scared.

But then I got a break. Somebody, a man, another trucker, stuck his head through the upper window-frame and extended his arms.

'Can you get him up this far?'

'Damn right,' I said between my teeth, and I flipped the driver's head and shoulders and arms backwards out of the bunk. I wedged myself under his lower back, with my shoulders flat against him and I stood up straight. I had most of him on my back. 'Bit more,' says the man up top, 'come on, baby, just a bit higher.' I gave another heave and did something to my back. I felt it go. I don't know that it'll ever be right again, right down at the bottom of the spinal column, an extruded disc. What a thing to have happen on a nice Tuesday morning. I stood right up straight and my back gave; there was pain, but the dead weight suddenly eased. The man on top got hold of him by the armpits and hauled on him. When the weight came away the pain in my back slacked off and I helped get him through the window. I don't know how they lowered him to the ground. Probably just dropped him over without waiting for ropes or nets; we were out of time. I got my left foot wedged into the space between the seat back and the cushions and worked my way up till I was supported by the steering wheel. That way I got my head and shoulders through the window.

Big crowd around, trucks and passenger vehicles on both sides of the median. When they saw me they started cheering and clapping their hands, but none of them thought to give me a hand to get down. I left my jacket in there. What good's a new pair of trousers without a jacket? Frances was crying. 'Get down,' she yelled, 'hurry up and get down.' Then people started running behind her, every which way.

I only saw the one flicker of fire. I almost felt like laughing when I saw them scatter like that, all but Fran. She stood there, right on the pavement below me. The OPP had blocked the right lane and were letting westbound traffic move slowly along the passing lane. They stopped the traffic when they saw the threat of fire. Made the provincials run like rabbits, I can tell you. My legs weren't working so good and I nearly dived down to the ground on my head while I was trying to get clear. I tried to support my body by bracing my hands on the window frame but it wouldn't work. Joints too stiff. So I crawled out as best I could, yanking myself along by the arms till I was lying on the frame of the hood and the fender. Smoke. Smoke!

I didn't wait any more. I just threw myself off and fell hard on the ground, jarred my jaw and broke a filling when my teeth snapped shut. You wouldn't think an eight-foot fall would shake you up like that. I didn't feel much like moving but suddenly I saw a real sheet of flame, not a flicker this time, blue and red, from somewhere under the rear suspension. I stood up and walked through a line of empty cars down into the median and along towards our car; then I turned around. I expected to see the kind of sight you see on the eleven p.m. news, one of those huge destructive fireballs, but it didn't materialize. Two OPPs came running up; they both carried big foam extinguishers, the ones with the trumpet-shaped nozzles. In about half a minute they had a mound of foam twenty feet high covering that rig, tractor and trailer both. You never saw anything like it, a great big sort of wedding cake or whipped cream topping or mound of shaving foam. It was pretty. Cream coloured and all streaked with yellow and full of bubbles. That's the thing I remember most about the incident, that big beautiful cake of foam.

They wouldn't let us go for hours, took down all the details, the times, the cause of the accident, our name and address and phone number in Montréal. We didn't get home till just before dinner time, and Frances had to drive all the rest of the way. I was starting to stiffen up and my lower back was hurting and I seemed to be having some kind of a reaction. I started to shake. My arms trembled and the muscles in my calves were twitching. It wasn't like me. I was sore for weeks afterwards. Investigators and insurance people, adjusters, and interviewers kept bothering us. Who was driving the passing car? Was the truck-driver in any way responsible for the crash? (Did they suppose I was going to finger him for them?) Exactly what time did the accident occur? What were the roadway and driving conditions? They wouldn't let us alone.

And then this morning I get this stupid letter. Frances opens the mail. We don't get much mail apart from the drugstore and grocery flyers and once in a while a note from Babette. Franny opens this letter and reads it and starts to bawl. Holds out the sheet of paper at me.

'Oh, George,' she says. There isn't much that'll make her cry. 'They're giving you an award, a medal, the Star of Courage. George, I'm so proud of you!'

I've been having nighttime trouble. 'Medal me no medals,' I said. 'I don't even want to think about it.'

Disappearing Creatures of Various Kinds

LEONORA PICCOLINA found a bird sitting on her woodpile, a nestling barely fledged, if fledged at all, and scarcely covered in a suit of greyish-brown feathers of microscopic proportions, tailless. The creature proclaimed its presence loudly, cheerfully, though in size about as big as a dustball or furball. Thoughts of fur gave place at once to thoughts of prowling cats. This chirping inchling would certainly attract the attention of the next cat to pass. The street was largely peopled with intense, hungry felines.

She folded the infant sparrow in one palm, then held it to the light with a lifting, wafting wave of the hand. The bird was supposed to reascend the skies, or at least to fly up into the rafters of the porch roof, where the maternal nest was well in sight. But the bird couldn't manage tailless flight, or do without the usual pre-flight instructions from parents. It remained seated on the lady's extended hand, eyeing her with bright tiny orbs which shifted to keep her in view as she swung her arm laterally. As she completed one of these motions, she reversed the direction of her arm too briskly, and the sparrow sailed off her palm into the air, there fluffing out its down and parachuting to the veranda floor beside the cordwood; it was almost lighter than air but it couldn't fly by itself.

So naturally there was nothing to do but bring it inside. Sitting it once more in the hollow between fingers and thumb, tickled by the scratchings of infinitesimal feet, she dawdled into her kitchen wondering what sort of commitment she was in process of forming. For of course her sympathetic action had implied a promise to the bird, a contract established. Eat or be eaten, she thought.

The idea was to nurture the creature until it would give evidence of ability to subsist independently: feed it up and free it. How do you feed something that size, she wondered; the bill was too small for a spoon. This judgement made her remember, idiotically, some jazzy number from the nineteen-forties. 'Your feet's too big for de bed.' Your bill's too small for de spoon. Dum dum diddle diddle want some seafood, Mamma. It was the young woman's habit to amuse herself with tuneful nonsense-songs as she roamed around the food-service centre preparing meals for this one or that one. There were three other birds in residence at that epoch.

She found an eye-dropper off the top of an empty bottle of bird vitamins. She washed it and rinsed it, then warmed some skimmed milk, testing it continually with her elbow. She had the new bird sitting in a roasting pan from which escape would be impossible unless true aviation were achieved. Anyway the bird didn't want to escape. It sat with every appearance of satisfaction in the middle of the roasting pan waiting – as had so many other beings in Leonora's personal history – to be fed, and fed plenty, and quick.

She held the tip of the eye-dropper gingerly over the sparrow's head; there was a bill or beak in there somewhere, about two centimetres long, barely visible. She poked at it with great care; it might be soft or breakable or not ready to be opened. Wasn't the bird just out of the egg? Wasn't some form of albumen still its preordained food, white of egg? She didn't have any information on the subject. The thing had hatched out after all; useless to try to reverse a natural process. Meanwhile the skimmed milk was cooling. She poked again at the tip of the forming bill and rejoiced to see it yawn wide, or as wide as anything that small could yawn, head well back, mouth gaping and still. In went the milk one drop at a time. A drop missed and drenched the poor creature. Bluish-white fluid spread through crest or comb.

Other experiments in feeding followed hard upon advice provided by the local branch of the SPCA. Egg-yolk in appreciable quantities, according to the voice on the telephone the most nutritious and digestible foody substance available for the feeding of such strays. These instructions puzzled Leonora, for was not the bird's own body composed of yolk of egg? Wouldn't it be feeding on something very like itself? Of course, said the telephone voice of the SPCA. It is in this that right nutrition consists, the eating of things as much like ourselves as can be found. Our bodies are meat. Therefore we should eat much meat and assimilate it the more perfectly to ourselves. There seemed to be something incorrect about this primitive view of nutrition.

'Wouldn't that mean that vegetarians turn into vegetables?'

'Well, and don't they?' inquired the telephone voice.

Whatever the rights and wrongs of these views, Leonora, herself a hearty consumer of meat and meat by-products, soups, stews, savouries, gravies, found them compelling. Turning chops and steaks into bits of herself – the bits that other people loved most – struck her as an entirely natural process, just as the sheep of the Scottish Highlands always struck her as instant-sweaters, mohair on the hoof. She lived a life sunk in primitive comparisons; this little bird needed bone-making material. What should she feed it but calcium? She started to mix a liquid dietary supplement in with the milk, a substance guaranteed to provide birds with sufficient daily dosages of all needed nutritional components: iron, calcium, riboflavin, the B-complex vitamins, much vitamin C, certain essential trace metals. She had to get up three times nightly during the bird's first week in residence to make sure that it hadn't stopped eating and died. 'Eats like a bird.' The most misleading cliché in the language. To eat like a bird is to eat all the time, to be forever in search of more food. In caged birds those ceaseless motions from swing to perch, from perch to water dish, from there to the cage-floor and back to upper perch, are instinctual imitatings of the endless search conducted by birds out there beyond the cage, free in the natural world to seek and seek until one day the hardly-maintained balance between energy output and nutritional intake fails, not enough is consumed to allow rest at night; the next day the exhausted bird falls behind the flock in the search, body temperature declines. Death ensues.

After a week of getting up nights she had the bright idea of moving the sparrow's cage into the sunroom next to the enormous condominium which housed her biggest bird, a splendid vigorous Patagonian conure with a rough edge to his tongue, very well-marked feeding and preening patterns, and a fundamentally good heart. This was an excellent notion, for the nestling immediately began to learn patterns of bird behaviour, drinking from its dish, consuming numberless grains of millet embedded in peanut-butter spread thickly on slices of whole-wheat. Once the feeding problem was licked, the sparrow went from strength to strength until it had mastered the entire curriculum of avian life: chirping, nesting in the paper at the bottom of the cage, drinking copiously at any moment, swinging on his little trapeze, biting at extended fingers. He liked to be allowed out of the cage from time to time, and could volplane erratically from the kitchen table to the floor. Unaided ascent from floor to table seemed however to exceed his powers. It always seemed to Leonora that he (or she?) had never achieved full growth, was not quite the size of the sparrows that flocked abundantly around the lilacs in the garden. And there was a design problem with the empennage. Were there quite enough feathers to get the job done? Who could tell? The creature flourished in all other respects; extended flight wasn't a given in its psychological horizons anyway.

We never know what fate holds in store. Leonora was obliged from time to time to travel to a city about 300 miles distant which held certain career opportunities for her. She usually flew over on Tuesdays, on an early-morning flight, returning on an evening flight the following day, which allowed two full working days out of town. At these times she used to hire the young girl who lived next door – a real sweetie who closely resembled the young Ginger Rogers – as a bird sitter, somebody to come in and feed and water the birds and chatter with them, cover their cages around ten-thirty p.m., and generally reassure the little things as to the continuance of their régime. This child adored the birds, socialized with them readily, and had picked up a considerable amount of parrot speech over two or three years. She was particularly fond of the little sparrow, which would perch on her forefinger and peck viciously at her thumb. She admired its resolution in self-defence while constrained by minute proportions.

Leonora flew off to take care of a career assignment one Tuesday, leaving this little girl in charge of the house and the birds. On the first day everything went forward routinely: tickling of the chattering lory behind the head and neck, brisk exchange of dialogue with the little green Brazilian conure which was the senior bird on strength, above all a chance for the sparrow to get out of its cage and strut back and forth on the kitchen counter. These amusements beguiled the whole of the first evening; the child was never bored by the birds. That night she assisted them to rest with food and water and soft cluckings and chirpings. All night perfect peace reigned in the house; she didn't have to come in until noon on Wednesday, when she uncovered the cages. A couple of the birds seemed to suspect that the night had been unusually long but their spirits appeared in no way dampened by protracted roost. They seemed full of beans, ready to converse, well-nourished, competitive in voice.

The young house-sitter expected Leonora back that evening around nine-fifteen. She watched some TV, prepared food for the birds and for herself, and allowed the sparrow out of his/her cage for a stroll. All at once the bird rose freely into the air impelled by vigorous wing-action, a wholly new achievement for him. Everybody just took it for granted that this bird was male; there was masculinity, even masculinism, in every point of its behaviour. Now it soared in an elegant arc off the edge of the counter, rising maybe three feet from its take-off point, then descending gracefully to the kitchen floor. The girl was transfixed; she made her mouth a big round o of wonder, and breathed out explosively.

'Well, I never....' The telephone rang urgently. It was Leonora, calling long-distance to say that she'd finished her assignment early in the day and would be taking a correspondingly early flight home.

'So you can expect me in at about seven,' she said rapidly.

Her sitter started to describe the sparrow's extraordinary action but was interrupted. '... calling my flight, got to run, 'bye now.'

She hung up the phone and tiptoed carefully back into the kitchen, careful not to tread on the presumably fatigued sparrow. But when she got there, the cupboard and everything else in the room was bare. No bird! Goodness, what a shock! The search began. Nowhere in the kitchen. Where then? Wandered into the dining-room? Most unlikely. Upstairs? When? Where? She raced to the second floor and searched earnestly and then to the attic, knowing that she was behaving desperately; the bird couldn't have made its way to the attic in the time elapsed. Not unless some invisible agency had powered its flight, which seemed unlikely. In great distress of mind, Ginger – we'll call her Ginger – went back downstairs to the kitchen where she scrutinized the empty cage, the floor, the skirting and baseboards, the cabinet under the sink where cleaning materials were stored, floor polish, Mr Clean, Drano. Not a trace of bird life.

She sat back on her hunkers and wept. What would Leonora say? She'd be home in a couple of hours and would consider that her small neighbour had betrayed her trust; useless to plead that her ill-timed phone call had caused unfortunate inattention. Tears trickled down her face. Wouldn't somebody intervene to clear her of this fault? Suddenly, among the restless cawings and chucklings of the other birds in the house, she heard the distinct individual cheepings of the vanished sparrow, the flutter of extended wings, scrabbling scraping noises, sounds of climbing. She felt along the baseboards in the direction of the pantry and sure enough there was an aperture where the baseboard turned the corner into the pantry recess. The boarding was of some stiff black plastic material which had sprung loose at the corner from its bond with the lowest lath. There was a hole there bigger than a mousehole, certainly wide enough to allow ingress to a very small bird.

She put her ear to the wall which divided pantry from kitchen; it wasn't a bearing wall, merely a partition inserted by the builders as an afterthought. There was unquestionably some living creature moving around inside between the lightly plastered surfaces. He'd walked through the hole and fluttered up between the wall surfaces, whether from panic or some misguided spirit of adventure it was not possible to judge.

Ginger stood up and leaned against the partition, lifting herself on her tiptoes and putting her ear to the plaster surface. She was a tall child, standing about five feet seven. She realized as she listened that the sparrow had attained a height about level with her ear. She felt an instant awful identification with the trapped creature; being in there would be like being buried alive. She whimpered, told herself that she was practically a grown woman, dashed her arm across her eyes, then burst into floods of tears and went next door to fetch her father. He, amazed, for Ginger was a courageous girl who hadn't cried publicly for a decade, followed her into Leonora's kitchen where he spotted the hole in the baseboard, the structural properties of the partition, and the loud noises which the sparrow was now creating in its amazed darkness. Only an hour or at most ninety minutes now remained before Leonora's return; it was clearly incumbent on them to get that darned bird out of there instanter. He tapped the walls; it might be necessary to breach them. The structure seemed lightly framed in. Perhaps a few blows with a wrecking bar...?

But no, they really couldn't greet their neighbour with the sight of a demolished pantry wall. What to do? How to entice the bird out of the terrifying dark? Cut a window-sized hole in the wall? Tricky, very tricky. He turned to his daughter and spoke emphatically.

'Go down to my workroom and get the big spotlight, not a flashlight, the one with the big red battery pack and the sealed-beam on top.'

Ginger grasped the situation in a flash and disappeared. In a few minutes she came back carrying the massive handsome object. Her father switched it on and placed it on its side, aimed so as to throw a bright beam into the hole at the baseboard.

'I'll set it to flash on-off, on-off,' he told Ginger. 'And we'll put seed and water just inside the hole.'

'Why not put the water just outside the hole?'

'Good thinking!' They placed their lures and settled down to wait. The other birds in the house fell silent, possibly alive to the state of emergency in the kitchen; the silence deepened as an hour went slowly by. Occasional chirpings from the wall suggested no change of position by the trapped bird. Leonora must be on her way in from the airport by now. Did she have her car, would she take a cab downtown or perhaps the bus? There wasn't much time left.

95

With half an hour to go they started to hear wing-noises, brushings, and the sound of loose bits of plaster raining down on the floor inside the partition. Could the bird be moving lower in its space? Yes! it was perceptibly descending towards the light. Father and daughter sat hugging one another and urging the bird downwards in their thoughts. The descent occupied fully thirty minutes as the small creature picked its way through various obstructions and finally fell with a thump to the floor beside the saucer of seeds that they had pushed inside. There were minute cracking sounds; the bird must be hungry, and if hungry then surely thirsty. They heard a car drive up and stand, motor running, outside the front door. Footsteps on the veranda, front door flung open and Leonora walked tiredly into the kitchen at precisely the same moment that her sparrow, tired, thirsty, draped liberally in cobwebs, cheeping in amazement at where he'd been, tottered out through the hole in the baseboard and began to drink copious drafts from his water dish. You could hear the liquid running down his throat.

'What in the world...?' exclaimed Leonora Piccolina.

Ginger gathered up the sparrow and returned him to safety. Then, bursting now and then into tears, she told her employer the whole story, sorrowful and hilarious at the same time, just like life.

'I can top that,' said Leonora fondly, looking at her rescued charmer, now swinging nonchalantly on his little trapeze, preening himself innocently as though he hadn't been out of the cage all day. While Ginger's Dad brought builder's-strength bonding agents and clamps, and with them sealed off the dangerous hole in the baseboard, she told the little girl the following tale.

This happened (she said) to a friend of mine, a schoolteacher in eastern Ontario of about my own age, a strong, canny, thrusting independent woman not about to be frightened easily or to imagine things which were not the case. One dark autumn night she was driving her car, a blue 1979 Plymouth, along old Highway 2 near the Kalahari Open Park Zoo, an institution long since closed. Just at that stretch of the highway, the road curves dangerously several times, rising and falling over a series of the rock ledges characteristic of that countryside. Swamp and slough lie between the upheaving rocks, and a series of small watercourses. Unpromising country, in late autumn somewhat sinister in tone.

She rounded sharp curve after curve, thinking of her bed, with perhaps a mug of steaming Ovaltine on the bedside table, and a few minutes' reading before putting the light out. The road ahead was indistinct, high rock ledges round about and no lights. Suddenly an immense dark form loomed up right in front of her. Before she could apply the brakes she collided with something dreadfully large and resistant. It was like driving head-on into an enormous stationary mattress, she said later. The car was stopped cold, and only her shoulder and waist seatbelts kept the lady from being pitched against the windshield, which might have caused serious, even perhaps fatal, injury. As it was, she managed to bump her chin against the steering wheel and sat stunned and senseless for at least three minutes and possibly longer.

She never knew who came to her aid, saw her stationary vehicle and alerted the police patrol. She doesn't to this day recall whether somebody passed her while she was sitting there in a state of blurred and darkened semi-consciousness. Everything seemed black. Then the flashing red and white turrets of a patrol car came into view and a pair of policemen pulled up on the opposite shoulder of the highway. They greeted her with truly brotherly solicitude, helped her out of the ruined Plymouth and gave rudimentary first aid; there was a painful blue bruise on the side of her chin and her neck and shoulders were very sore.

'Can you walk, miss? Why not go and sit in the patrol car, and we'll scout around and try to find out what happened. What was it you hit?'

'Or hit you?' added the other, younger officer, mindful of the possibility of lawsuits, court appearances and unprejudiced testimony. He took out a notebook and began to prepare a careful account of the accident while his superior examined the Plymouth, flashing a bright beam of light over the stove-in front end. After a moment or two he emitted a sigh of satisfaction and came back across the road.

'Just sit nice and easy in the back, ma'am,' he suggested, 'while I pull over onto the other shoulder. I want to get my headlights aimed at your grille.'

This evolution occupied about ninety seconds. The powerful headlights of the patrol car illuminated the collapsed grille and fenders and bumper and headlight housing and the abused tie-rod ends of the Plymouth as though it were high noon. A remarkable stamped-out shape or impression became visible in the body metal of the wreck.

'What do you make of that?' said the senior policeman to his assistant.

'Sir,' he replied, 'it's that damn hippopotamus again.' And certainly the impression stamped in the front of the car had the form or image of the great beast. The confidential exchange between the officers, and the strangeness of their remarks, alarmed the teacher who felt her usual poised confidence much undermined. She wept noisily while they tried in vain to comfort her.

'You're in no danger, ma'am; he'll be two or three miles from here by now, and anyway he isn't vicious, just slow-moving and heavy. This happens every now and then on a kind of cyclical basis. We've warned the zoo-keeper repeatedly, but there isn't any kind of fencing will keep that hippo out of action when the mood comes on him. We reckon it's love.'

For some reason this observation moved the lady to further tears. There was little the police officers could do except to run her down to the Emergency and afterwards, very late at night, to escort her to her apartment and make the Ovaltine. The arms and shoulders had stiffened. It was hard for her to hold her mug steady, so the younger officer held it to her lips and helped her to drink.

'You're being so kind to me,' she said drowsily. 'Can you do something about my car?' She gave them a signed authority and they arranged for towage into town on the following day, before they went off shift. Their helpfulness impressed the lady strongly. In the months to come she dated the younger policeman repeatedly. He used to come to her apartment and drink Ovaltine with her ... but that is another story.

The hippopotamus from the Kalahari Open Park Zoo had

indeed escaped; this wasn't the first time either. The owner had been given warning that further hippopotamine escapades would involve the possibility of licence-loss. It wasn't that the animal broke things or attacked people. Nobody knew what he ate when he went into the slough or how he busied himself when he got there, but folks were frightened. What about that auto accident, that schoolteacher? Middle of the night! Might happen to anybody. There was talk of posses with nets and shotguns or stunguns charged with pellets of powerful tranquillizers, to which the zoo-keeper objected vigorously.

'You don't have no idea,' he swore, 'how those drugs might take him. He's emotionally over-excited as it is. It's his time, if you fol-low me.'

The young woman television interviewer to whom he was talk-ing at the time averted her eyes modestly and changed the subject. The biological cycle of the male hippopotamus was perhaps an improper topic for public debate, although she herself felt a tremor of curiosity about it. She went on to lead the exchange into a discus-sion of the zoo's future, which seemed paradoxically both bright and dark.

'Attendance has skyrocketed for the time of year,' said the zoo-keeper, 'but the licensing authorities are dumping all over me. We've got to get that hippopotamus out of the swamp or slough. But how?'

How indeed, thought the interviewer, and she faced the camera with an intense plea for public assistance, for instant report of fur-ther sightings. The zookeeper and the TV station between them posted a substantial reward which was afterwards supplemented by the Stoverville *Intelligencer*. A host of conflicting reports poured in but nobody seemed inclined to follow them up. A hippo might weigh a couple of tons, and what if he rolled on you, somewhere out there in the swamp? Could be trouble!

Matters rested there for another week, down into early November, and then one night came the key break in the case. A middle-aged farm labourer, Charlie Vandermeulen, who lived a mile up the highway from the scene of the original accident, gave his mind fully to the circumstances of the story and drew an obvious conclusion. Out there somewhere the poor creature was seeking a mate. Where would he go, what would he do? What were the natural instincts in play?

As he said later, Charlie then tried to put himself in the hippopotamus's shoes. If he were a hippopotamus and he was out looking for a girl, where would he head for? That's easy, he'd head down into the creek and work along the banks and the fords where the vegetation was thick and lush. He would give his call and listen for responses. When he heard them he would head in that direction.

There was a creek in the neighbourhood, the Lyn creek, with a well-watered flow, which joined another watercourse a mile lower down, to create a sizeable river. The banks of the Lyn Creek are heavily freighted at all seasons with moist leafage. You might meet an occasional otter in there. Herons nest nearby in high pines.

Charlie set out with his twenty-year-old son one night around Armistice Day, driving down the highway a mile or so, hiking over huge rocky humps and sliding down mossy carpets to the recesses of the Lyn Creek. Once arrived at a location chosen arbitrarily, or imaginatively – not quite the same thing – he began to give out with a series of long and plangent wailings in a musical sequence which suggested a pentatonic mode. His son listened with amazement; he had never suspected his father of any such talent. There was an undeniable appeal to these outcries, expressive, attractive, and in a curious way inviting and even seductive. For a time there was no other sound but the whistling of the night wind. But then, suddenly, the two men heard a tremendous sucking sound, like the noise which a mammoth rubber plunger might make in some leviathan of a sink. The huge flanks and shoulders of the runaway hippopotamus manifested themselves under the November moon. Charlie and his boy felt awe and admiration at the sight.

'Get back to the car and get the OPP on the CB. Tell them we've located him. Tell them to bring nets. Say we claim the reward. I'll stay here and keep calling to him.' The young man obeyed his father promptly, slinking away through the underbrush so as not to alarm their quarry. He reached the roadway in a few minutes and ran to where they had parked. He had no trouble raising the OPP on the CB. At that period the provincials monitored the Citizens Band carefully, listening for appointments between traffickers and users. When they heard about the hippo sighting, their SWAT team sped into action; the armoured car, the tear-gas canisters, the rubber bullets and stun pellets, the nets, their whole array of anti-terrorist equipment, gas masks, huge steel helmets of debased design, long and cruel batons. There may have been an element of overkill in their preparations.

They zipped down the highway to the rendezvous with young Vandermeulen, picking him up readily in the glare of many floodlights. Some of the officers grumbled at the distance they were forced to traverse over rock and through the slough to the sighting-point. They hoped that this was not a false alarm. When they had gotten near Charlie's improvised hippopotamus-blind they halted and listened, and heard a remarkable exchange, the languorous invitations emitted by the cunning farm labourer and in response a sequence of vast yearning sighs, the lover's complaint of an impassioned and famished river horse (Gk., *hippos*, horse; *potamos*, river), a sound which mollified and persuaded these determined men in a graceful and soothing way. They took the great animal prisoner very easily, he making no resistance to their casts of nets. They showed him food, suggested warmth and security, and he came forth. By this time the ubiquitous TV crew from Kingston was on the scene, including their powerful young woman interviewer who ordered that the capture be re-enacted twice so that the moment could be preserved on colour videotape. She then interviewed Charlie at length, arriving at last at the crucial questions.

'And how did you come to guess where he was?'

'Just tried to put myself in his place. Where would you go if you were a hippopotamus and you were feeling sexy?'

The interviewer dimpled. 'Would you like to share that secret with our viewers?'

'Course I would. You'd go looking in the nearest swamp, or slough.'

'And just how did you initiate dialogue with him?'

'I just, like, imitated the mating call of the female hippopotamus.'

'Well, but how did you happen to know it?'

'I didn't know it,' said Charlie. 'I made it up.' And so (concluded Leonora) we see that our sympathies can reach out and touch all creatures from the largest to the very least. She smiled at Ginger, opened the cage door and invited the sparrow with her twinkling fingers. The bird seemed to kiss the beckoning hand.

In this way our lives radiate allegories and symbols at all times.

Last Remake of Nosferatu

1: SIGNORA NERITTINI moved as though in a trance past the reception desk and into the shadowed hall, tripping over Bruno whose massive rump protruded from beneath a rush-bottomed chair. The old dog stirred in his sleep and began to wheeze awfully, the body alternately inflated and deflated by struggle for breath. The *padrona* crossed herself as the wheezes and gasps mounted in volume, then suddenly stopped, leaving echoes of animal distress volleying around the dusty salons and galleries of the Albergo Santo Spirito. Nothing could now be done for Bruno, whose last hour had been at hand for many months; he woke, drank, mouthed some questionable morsel of veal, rejected it, slept again, frequently exploding in sequences of terrifying digestive noises and pulmonary near-crises.

The signora paused briefly in her dark lobby, then passed decisively into a handsome, well-lighted dining room whose tables might accommodate fifty guests seated according to the form of a capital E with the central bar omitted in such a way as to allow every diner sight of the Chianti hills as they rose up in choppy waves around Montalto. The broad range of windows faced roughly east towards the height of land which divided Val d'Elsa from Val d'Arno, terrain bitterly disputed from the twelfth to the fifteenth century. The spirits of hundreds of discontented citizen soldiers from contesting city-states, Sienese, Florentine, hovered sempiternally above the small hill towns, attracted and stimulated no doubt by the rising intoxicating odour of the classic Chianti grape.

On this afternoon the spacious dining salon stood empty, dust-ridden, deserted alike by the living and the sanctified. Although fifty covers lay set and ready along tables hewn from the great oaks of the district (her brother-in-law's family name was Querciagrossa) none of the places had been disturbed perhaps for many previous days. The carefully-folded napery, the dully-gleaming cutlery, had the air of long situation in their present positions. The room resembled the setting for an opera based upon the tragic erotic attachments of the *contado*, loves of the Nerittini, Querciagrossi, Castellini. Act One, Scene One, the banqueting room in the castle.

From the adjacent kitchens came the sounds of rushing streams of water and of wine. They would be refilling the *fiaschi* against the slender possibility of the hotel's recommencing operation at some future time. She had given orders for this hopeful act. Bruno had lingered for months, anything might yet happen. She might yet find the Albergo Santo Spirito flooded with unwelcome guests. For had not a pair of transients forced their way into the reception room two days before and insisted in halting and inexpressive Italian, understanding nothing of her disclaimers, upon reserving a room for this night and the next? She went in terror of losing her licence to operate. Her long-dead sister's spouse would never survive such a forfeiture. The Albergo Santo Spirito was all their children and all their lovers too. She was obliged to accept guests as they came, so the *fiaschi* must be refilled.

Her major-domo, Giancarlo, and the kitchenmaid, a nameless creature from the depths of the nearby town of Querciagrossa, shrieked joyfully as the bottling machine rotated, its mechanical tongues and sealers swinging round and round, the freshly rinsed bottles parading neatly under the reservoir of new wine, then emerging, each one corked without the intervention of disease-ridden human hands. They rattled down a chute at the rate of about one a minute to a marble-topped pastry table where Giancarlo gathered them in his arms and ran to distribute them along ranks of perhaps purely imaginary diners. The signora listened impatiently to the bump and rattle of the straw-covered flasks and reflections about new wine and old bottles rose unbidden to her mind.

'Set wine out on the terrace,' she commanded Giancarlo when he returned, arms empty, from the dining salon.

'Wine for three parties?'

'For every table,' declared Signora Nerittini. She would display her new wine like a gonfalon, a ruby-tinted flag of defiance. There were twelve tables on the terrace. If this were to be the very last night of all – she gritted her teeth – she would have the terrace lighted up, would herself count over the eleven tortoises of varying sizes who had lived there since she was a tiny girl. Perhaps they were not precisely the same eleven but their number remained constant. She would display them for the evening's guests; the tortoises would remain after the guests had departed.

Giancarlo filled his wide arms with flasks and trotted away to the other side of the building, into the sloping garden which hung almost in mid-air, perched next to the sharp drop towards Montalto Basso, the despised lower town inhabited by railway hands and Communist Party officials, hereditary enemies of the dwellers on the high hill. Montalto Basso, she thought, ridiculous name! Tears rose in her eyes as she contemplated her spirited major-domo, the pretty garden, the long-disused, ivy-overgrown wellhead, the bulging terra-cotta urns, here and there a slow tortoise engaged upon some purposive excursion. Short journeys, immensely protracted, towards imponderable destinations.

Turning away from her prospect of the terrace, she mounted the wide staircase, footsteps echoing under the high ceilings; every space in the albergo rang and answered to her movements. Arrived at the upper floor she peered apprehensively along the marbled corridor that led to the guest accommodation. Nothing moved or sounded in that direction. The chambermaid had dusted the rooms some time ago and had spent the days since in caring for the signora's poor brother-in-law who lay exhausted and inert, dark-faced, silent on the grand bedstead in the signora's own quarters in the west wing.

Signora Nerittini slunk away from the guest wing towards the great black oak doors which barred entry to her own rooms. There she turned the massive pair of black iron rings which actuated the latches, and hauled the doors partly open, to be greeted by the sound of wailing and sniffling, and by slow laboured breathing. She passed through her brother-in-law's bedchamber – till lately her own – and emerged on a little balcony beneath which all approaches to Montalto lay open to inspection, the railway line and the trackage north and south, the correspondent highway with its never-ending stream of traffic, then the cruel winding ascent of the local road from valley along hillside up to the walls of the hilltop town, 1200 years old, lord of the vineyards, immune from attack by foot soldier, Montalto.

It was by now mid-afternoon. She stared downwards at the difficult ascending track. Far below, perhaps 450 feet straight down, two persons, man and woman, stood uncertainly at the outwards edge of the road, her guests for tonight. Why had the fools walked from the station? Would they succeed in their climb? It would be better not.

Re-entering the darkened bedchamber she realized that the sniffling attendant had vanished, leaving in her mistress' charge her only relative, her expiring brother-in-law. He didn't move, cheeks pulsing slowly in and out, the huge moustache rising up and relapsing like some surprising marine growth moved by tidal drift, puff, suck, in, out. As she watched, the rise and fall grew slower, showing less amplitude. In ... out ... in ... out ... in. The massive skull lay couched among her finest pillows. Who could judge what final pains might torment the stricken brain? Out ... in ... out.... A bell rang sharply at a distance and Bruno gave a low surprised moan.

2: THREE-WHEELED, underpowered, gasping like humble draft animals, donkeys or ponies bred among these straitened hills and at last exhausted by a lifetime of toil, the Piaggio camionnettes endemic to the region crept upwards past Luke and Meriel Springford. Husband and wife struggled spasmodically in heated motion towards the brick and terra-cotta citadel that dominated the crumbling hill town, the steep vineyards and the new town below.

'Oh, couldn't we catch one of those smelly little things, hitch a ride, throw the bags in the back? Why wasn't there a taxi anywhere? What a climb! Oooofff!' Meriel stopped abruptly, bent and squeezed each plump thigh alternately between strong pressing palms. 'My poor legs!' She turned her back briefly on the citadel and advanced to the verge of the roadway, just at the edge of the drop through vines towards the valley. She put a shadowing hand to her forehead and squinted at the prospect of S. Gimignano twenty-five miles to the northwest. The thirteen towers of that stunning hill site stood up before her like the fingers of the buried dead grasping at the sun. Luke, she saw, hadn't scrupled to expend yet more of their travelling time, though it was now mid-afternoon and the sun glared at them full-face. Siesta time. There would be nothing moving in the town for another two hours. No wonder they had found no taxi near the station. She remembered that taxi operators notoriously bedded with their patronesses between two-thirty and five; the matter was almost dictated in their official licences. The next train from Siena to Empoli wasn't due until four-fifteen.

Luke had located his smaller sketchbook and was – she told herself grimly – limning the brilliant scene with swift deft strokes. She gritted her teeth and almost shed tears as yet another tricycle pickup went by at eight miles an hour, negotiated the difficult bend that impended nearby, and disappeared. She could hear its load of empty bottles dancing and chiming as the miniature engine strained and stuttered and strained again. They might have thrown their baggage into the vehicle, instructed the driver to off-load it at the Albergo Santo Spirito, and thereby been relieved of their worst burdens. She had the uneasy feeling that their hotel wasn't where it ought to be, that it wouldn't be discoverable at the fag-end of town where the walls faded into air, hanging in the difficult sky mirage-like. The towers of S. Gimignano now appeared to number only eleven; two had melted into the afternoon shimmer.

But who's counting, she asked herself. Behind her, Luke snapped his sketchbook shut, inserted it in his single piece of luggage, took up his companion's burden and his own and began once more the trying ascent. The back of his fine cotton shirt was dark with sweat, Meriel saw; he was no longer a very young man. She might just shoulder her own luggage for a time, but when she tried to relieve Luke he resisted her.

'It's nothing,' he insisted, sighing with fatigue. And then bravely, 'I got us into this and I'll get us out.' Meriel made no reply, following the tottering man around the bend to the left onto a last stretch of roadway above which the town unfolded like a poppy, exhaling forgetfulness into three o'clock.

But then, which way was their hotel? Up or down? They found themselves standing exactly in the middle of the only true roadway in the place, which ran along the spine of the hilltop west to east where the *piazza principale* stretched out its small space between church and nobleman's feudal retreat.

'It wasn't anywhere near the square,' said Luke in perplexity. 'We've gotten turned right round. It has to be down the street at the other end.' He lurched away in front of her, plainly relieved to be descending the Avernian slope; he was right in his conjectures. In moments a tiny placard announced the entryway to the Albergo Santo Spirito, and the odorous airs which wafted from an enclosed garden at their right hand confirmed the declaration. They rang, opened the door, heard an answering ring from some bell actuated by the opening door, then no further sound until they were startled almost out of their wits by an unearthly groan and a dreadful smell of corruption, of radical animal indigestion. Looking to the left they observed the hindquarters of an ancient dog, almost invisible under a chair. The dog emitted a series of hacking, throat-clearing coughs, but did not attempt to come near them or even to rise. And still no human person showed in the recesses of the reception room. What was to be done? Luke dredged up from a trouser pocket the little card upon which the signora had pencilled the dates of their reservation. He studied it with foolish bewilderment.

Together they moved across the room to the doors which lay open on their right. Here was the delightful terrace that housed a legion of creeping creatures. Taking Meriel by the hand, Luke led her out into the garden where a world lay all before them; they crossed to the sunwards side and sank to rest on a low wall. Below them some three hundred feet a pair of vineyard workers were doing something with mattock and spade. 'Dig it and dung it,' murmured Meriel, having no faintest notion what she intended by the phrase. At her feet a smallish tortoise – or turtle, what was the difference – began to crawl into a pie-pan filled with what looked like lettuce leaves a little browned at the edges. Another tortoise (turtle?) hove in view along the curve of the wall. They sat eyeing the noiseless creatures. Would nobody tell them what was happening? In silent agreement they seated themselves at one of the small red wooden tables distributed around the garden. More formal tables arranged for dining stretched past them under a sheltering tiled roof. Meriel smiled at the sight of a long rank of Chianti flasks; somebody must be here to bottle and consume the famous wine of the district, the Columbus of wines. They would certainly dine well; they were not to be rushed or crowded. If only somebody would show them to their room.

And somebody finally did. An intermittently jovial major-domo or maître d'hôtel now came towards them from the interior of the building and made a sequence of remarks which sounded like firecrackers to their untuned ears. Meriel could read the language but was unable to speak it or grasp its rhythms when spoken to her. Luke stood in scarcely better case. He could express simple requests for food, for accommodation, for information, in understandable Italian, but like his companion found great difficulty in deciphering rapid response. So there ensued one of those comic interludes of crosstalk by which their Italian travels were so often punctuated. Finally Giancarlo – they had collected his name from the ruins – dragged them to a desk where Luke inscribed their names on an empty page of a large old album. They received a key made of black cast-iron and were directed by an expressive arm to a row of rooms dimly visible along a corridor at the top of the splendid staircase. No nonsense about attention to their luggage which they were plainly required to juggle for themselves. The dog stank!

At the top of the stairs forward progress was impeded by a pair of gloomy black oak doors with huge old rings depending from their heavy locks. From below a vigorous old voice chanted solemnly 'A destro, a destro.' They turned and proceeded along a high-ceilinged, marble-floored passage as far as they could go. Here they came upon a door that bore the same number as their key. Setting down their heavy pieces of luggage they cast open this door and found themselves in a grandiose corner suite, with writing room or study, stately bathroom, isolated WC, bedchamber fitted with ancient armoires, immense shuttered windows, a vast canopied bed, and a thick layer of fine dust which might have lain there for the whole term of an enchantment. Prising open the shutters proved difficult; they operated on some complex system for simultaneously rolling them up and spreading them apart. Luke spent half an hour finding out how they moved, pinching his fingers so cruelly as to draw blood on two separate occasions. Finally he achieved a modest aperture, some flow of ventilation. Dust rose like smoke in the wide room; from the monstrous bathroom came snorts of steam, gurgling of pipes, clanking noises.

When Meriel debouched from the bath chamber she was a modified carmine in hue, alteration of ordinary pigmentation which seemed weirdly appropriate, given the other-worldly atmosphere of the place. They drew down the bed coverings and lay together at the very end of the siesta hour, chuckling together over the peculiarities of their lodgings.

'Not a living soul in sight!'

'Except for the doorkeeper. Will they serve meals, do you think?'

'I fancy I can hear some sort of preparations going on.'

This was so. Occasional snatches of song, footsteps, scrapings of chair legs on cold stone floors, intimated the progress of some form of kitchen activity. Sometimes these signals were interrupted, sometimes wholly obscured, by tubercular retchings and strangulated heaves which might have been either human or canine. The invisible high ceilings and the chilly flooring magnified these horrid sounds and caused them to reverberate along the Springfords' corridor like echoes from a naval engagement fought at a vast distance.

'Are we going to get up?'

'Ought we to take some exercise before dining?'

'We might walk right round the hilltop, just to fix the topography in our minds; this is one of the most celebrated of the hill towns. It's in all the books.'

They sighed in unison; tourism sometimes fails.

All the same, they dragged themselves out of the billowing mattresses towards six in the evening, dressed in fresh clothes and sallied downstairs, through the reception room and out the front door. It surprised them to see that the sun still shone high and bright in the west. In the next hour they walked completely around the hilltop, following overgrown paths below and behind stained and overgrown cellars and foundations. Sometimes their route took them out to the last edge of the slopes, where they were able to gaze away into the first green tints of moonrise, over across the piled-up small hills towards Firenze. As they sauntered around the eastern shoulders of Montalto hints of daylight realism, the ordinary and credible, began to mould the scene. Living voices, the tones, well satisfied with life and with themselves, of a couple of dozen Swiss and German travellers whose Mercedeses and BMWs revealed themselves to our hiking couple as they rounded a final turn and re-entered the maze of building at the extreme east end of the site.

There appeared to be some sort of upscale *trattoria* or *ristorante* tucked away in the ancient fastnesses of the counts of Montalto, patronized as it seemed by folks who came for meals from great distances but who did not choose to remain in the town for a single night. Luke and Meriel viewed the ranks of luxurious automobiles with great disfavour as they picked their way among them. They told each other that they were far better off at their chosen hotel. No doubt the fare at the Albergo Santo Spirito would far outgo so-called gourmet dining events to be encountered among these Germans and yodellers. Hand in hand our adventurers walked the length of the main thoroughfare, nodding and smiling approvingly at one another as they sighted the delightful garden adjoining their hotel. They entered, were greeted by Giancarlo and led straightaway to a neat inviting table halfway along the garden terrace. By gesture and in staccato speech he indicated that they would have no sight of their hostess during the meal, but that everything would be carried out according to her personal instructions to ensure their comfort, their pleasure.

A sense of the unreal which had been gaining on them through the late afternoon and the lemony-green twilight was partially dissipated by observation of the other two parties disposed at tables not distant from their own. Towards the lowest depths of the garden a pair of young lovers, touring motorcyclists by their appurtenances, gazed into each other's eyes and spoke little, and that suggestive.

Immediately next to Meriel and Luke, three Englishmen, two young and the other perhaps sixty, rattled away in an interminable chat which cruelly ignored the existence of their surroundings. Some question about the administration of a college or institute attended by the younger men, directed perhaps by the elder, absorbed their energies entirely, so that they heard nothing else and neither did they see Luke, Meriel, the mooning motorcyclists, their food, the eleven peripatetic tortoises or turtles which paraded around in the evening light like souls undergoing purgation in some half-world. Ah, the self-absorbed arrogance of the English academic officer. Where would the world be without it?

'There is no difference,' said the elderly gent at the next table, betraying momentary attention to his surroundings, 'though some confine one usage to land creatures, the other to those of the sea. They're equally Old French, "tortue".'

Meriel and Luke eyed one another impishly, a mystery, one among many, resolved!

They emptied a first flask of the hotel's own wine, then found when they asked about a second that unlimited wine was a starry feature of the hotel's meal service. Result: they went handsomely drunk to bed, exhilarated by the copious drafts which were completely out of their customary line of behaviour. They had to help one another up the stairs, pausing unsteadily at the top long enough to scrutinize various dubious curios which were displayed along their corridor: oaken tables topped with questionable travertine or lapis, alabaster busts a long way after Bernini, a couple of crossed lances and a hauberk or two.

'Ariosto,' giggled Luke.

'More like Coppola,' mumbled Meriel.

They fell among mattresses, attempted lovemaking briefly, and sank into uneasy slumber from which they awoke sometime past two in the morning; wailings, lamentations, the sound of hurried echoing footsteps, troops of persons coming and going on the stairs. They clutched at each other in the darkness, half terrified, half overcome with ungracious laughter. Towards dawn uneasy repose enveloped them and they slept late. When they emerged into mid-morning they were greeted at once by a stranger, male, tiny, bent, dressed in a grey suit cut originally for some much larger person, who informed them haltingly that they must go elsewhere for their meals during the remainder of their stay. Who he was, what his authority might be, was veiled in uncertainty. Behind him in recesses lying near the kitchen, under the stairway and behind the reception desk, a clump of weeping women in grey and black, heads nodding like clockwork toys, defined a tragic, Goyaesque background.

'*Non posso cenar, la sera?*'

'*Impossibile!*'

'*E la prima colazione?*'

'*No, no, no, e finita. Il cognato della padrona, signor, il fratello mio....*' Distracted gestures and tears.

Naturally Meriel demanded to know what that was all about, as soon as they were well clear of the building, from which lamentations and maledictions continued to swell.

'What in the name of God...?'

'All I did was ask about dinner.'

'And?'

'WELL! You saw! I think he put a curse on me or something. Maybe he thinks I've got the evil eye. No breakfast either, damn it.'

'We'll walk down to the station,' said Meriel, 'and enjoy our rolls and jam in peace and harmony.'

'*Cognato,* said Luke wonderingly, mispronouncing the word. 'I wonder what that means.' He had misheard the word and couldn't find it in his pocket dictionary.

'We'll combine breakfast with lunch,' said Meriel.

They combined the meals with great effect, beginning with *briocci* and continuing without any interval into *panini* and a series of cups of murderously strong espresso. By siesta time they found themselves in a state of radical wakefulness, no question of silken retirement; besides they were miles away from their hotel. Having walked out into fields two or three miles north of Montalto they discovered that no matter how they circled the base of the hill they couldn't spot the Albergo Santo Spirito. It simply wasn't to be seen from any viewpoint lying to the north of the townsite; this was very peculiar because they would both have sworn that the entortoised garden and the dining terrace looked directly down towards where they now stood.

Late in the afternoon, having sweated out the espresso, they turned back and began a very slow climb up the hillside. They'd come here expecting to lounge happily for forty-eight hours in the precise atmosphere of the early fourteenth century. Now they were impatient to be gone, and had the evening and another night to get through. There was difficulty too in finding the upscale dining place at the other end of the town. It wasn't until the small squadron of expensive automobiles started to slide silently up the hill and along the *via centrale* that they managed to locate this retired and exclusive restaurant which was, it appeared, attached to the only functioning hotel in the place, the Toscana, perched on a jutting prominence at the easternmost part of the place. Having no *prenotazione*, they had to persuade the staff to let them come in, and at last they were made to feel most unwelcome because of a slip in conversation with the proprietress of the hotel.

'... and they directed us here from the Santo Spirito,' said Luke mendaciously, thinking that this might serve as a reference. Their hostess recoiled with a sharp intake of breath. 'What are you telling me?'

'That's where we are staying.'

'But signor, I do not understand. There is no one at the Albergo Santo Spirito. No one has stayed there for many years.' She waved an agitated arm. An under-servant brought their bill, which the hostess then dramatically tore into small pieces.

'You go now,' she said. 'No, no,' as Luke offered his Visa card, 'I will accept nothing from you. I only ask you to leave.'

They had only just started on the *primo piatto!* So they were left dinnerless and amazed, and had to creep back and let themselves into their darkened hotel without information or assistance of any sort. Meriel carried three apples and a morsel of Bel Paese in her shoulder bag; they made a scanty late-night snack out of what they had and went to bed in a state of alarm and apprehension, clutching each other protectively, affectionately, and then passionately. Sometime past midnight they dropped into qualified and uneasy oblivion which was banished hours later by the tollings nearby of some massive bell, its measured strokes plainly funereal ... the passing bell. There were louder whispers in the dark, footsteps, cries and sobs, and finally a long mournful howl which went on and on and on. They rose in the dark, huddled themselves into their clothes, made every preparation for speedy departure and sat wrapped in one another's arms, peering through the wide-open windows in the direction of the dawn.

3: NEVER MIND FOOD, never mind asking questions, let's be gone. They tiptoed down the central staircase, Luke fingering a small wad of ten-thousand-lire notes which he intended to deposit on the reception desk as they passed through; the sum proposed would surely be enough. They had received no service or attendance of any kind, barring a single evening meal. But nobody leaves the Albergo Santo Spirito without paying exactly what is due. As Luke dropped the money on the desk, the small grey person of the day before arrested them, handed over an accounting meticulous in its calculations, waited while Luke added the required amount to his proposed settlement, then uttered further broken sounds of sorrow and distress. Scufflings and thumps drifted out from behind a screen; the major-domo and an old old creature of indeterminate sex now passed through the room towards the place where the fleshy rear of a deceased animal displayed itself under a chair. They shovelled the body, which must have weighed thirty-five pounds, onto an improvised hurdle or stretcher, and disappeared wordlessly. An awful odour trailed in their path.

'Anche Bruno ... è il mio fratello....'

The grey man took the money and disappeared.

It wasn't until they were halfway down the precipitous descent to the lower town that they worked it out. 'That man's brother was the owner's brother-in-law. *Cognato*. Brother-in-law. That's what it was.'

Meriel said, 'Was it the brother-in-law that died? Or the dog? Or both?'

'It must have been both: surely they wouldn't toll the passing bell just for old Bruno! Or would they? Must have been the brother-in-law.'

'Never buy life insurance from your brother-in-law,' said Meriel.

The Springfords continued their descent, and just as they moved off they overtook a dignified procession of eleven tortoises headed in the same direction.

Jill's Disappearing Nipples

NOBODY EVER FIGURED BRONSON for some kind of pervert or pornographer. He was if anything frightened by sexual display, irregular invitation, and had never been able to insinuate himself into the exhibition of even the softest-core dirty movie. There were two rundown theatres in the neighbourhood, the Pussycat and *le Sexe-au-coin*, offering change of blue movie weekly, sometimes oftener. Where did they get all those films, he wondered as he sidled past the crumbling marquees? Sometimes he crossed the street to avoid involuntary inspection of explicit posters. Were the production centres more actively employed in porn production than in turning out A-rated or even PGA material? He would like to have seen a dirty movie but it wasn't a pressing need; he had survived into his middle, even his later years, without deviating into porn use. Use. A user.

He was familiar with this conception from quasi-sociological studies prominent in the magazines which came into the house. *Homemaker. The Canadian Forum.* The Bronsons no longer paid much attention to the media but *Homemaker* came free and the *Forum* was the result of an interminable subscription purchased for addressee as a Christmas present by some long since forgotten sunk-without-trace associate. In the pages of these periodicals the phrase 'pornography use' often turned up together with certain variants and modifications. You had your hard-core use and your soft-core use and your inner-city trafficker. The innocent phrases suggested that the implied materials, skin books, dirty movies, articles vended in sex boutiques and ladies' lavatories, were commodities like any others. Drug use. French postcards ... feelthy postcards. Sometimes a comic song of immense antiquity rose up in memory to make him grin.

Buy my feelthy postcards!
They're far far feelthier than most cards,

And they've all been smuggled past the coastguards....

Who was it used to sing that? Wasn't it perhaps Danny Kaye? There was a tang of Tom Lehrer but it wasn't a Lehrer song, being at once insinuating and faintly leering. Anyway it seemed that in the *fin-de-siècle* world you could use pornography the same way you used soap or your deodorant; you applied it to your skin and it did you good.

There was the question of the various plastic-covered magazines elevated to the top shelves in the book and newspaper boutique at a neighbouring mall. These demure publications, far distant from the exploring paws of toddlers, were said to show a remarkable variety of tone and production value, ranging from slick through sleaze to clinical and at last vilely degraded. From *Penthouse* to shithouse, as it might be.

Quail, Flair, Grenadier, various expensive British publications celebrating the Nanny or the governess, the Teddy-bear, the pinafore, and then *Skin Boys, Jock Itch,* and other manuals of imperfectly heterosexual allegiance, their sister organs like *Fur, Areola,* and *Cleft,* were all too vividly displayed up there at the top of the shelving. Now and then Bronson's eyes might fall on a cover photo which had the distinctness of dream image partially obscured by the tight clear film of protective covering. Things which he had never looked at in his life took silvery form under the blurring shroud and suddenly became intelligible. Bronson would actually blush deeply – in his late forties – and edge along the row of shelves towards the piles of smeared grey newspapers and the eye-level racks which housed *Cosmopolitan* and *Saturday Night.* If he had had the nerve to lay his hands on one of the high hard mags he would have been daunted by its price, closer and closer to ten dollars.

Ten dollars for what? The uses of porn. He used many commodities but had never been a 'user' in the technical sense, an addict whose addiction was excused by the neutral word. Alcohol use. Coke use.

What, he often wondered, did feminists make of porn? Inasmuch as the culture seemed to permit innocent porn use, that is, for if the stuff was morally neutral upon what grounds might these deserving women base their objections to it? They might as well object to butter or pepper or ripe olives, say, or meat-eating or any other taste, and there could be no sort of moral or ethical objection to a taste. If you liked looking at photos of naked women, chained up and dangling from the branches of stunted trees, the worst that could be alleged about you was that you were one of a statistically determinate minority.

Bronson considered himself as normal as the next person, interested in a perfectly conventional way in the appearance of the naked female human form divine (Blake). He responded even now to imaginings of womanly beauty and felt confused by this or that group's objections to such representations. In a non-moral world – the statistical world – what were the grounds for any such objection? He enjoyed thinking about the forms of the female body, and would have dismissed any attempt to force him to surrender the habit. If no such imaginings are permissible, he argued with himself, what becomes of the urge to generation? How stimulate it? How persuade young men and women to act on it and accept the consequences with dignity? If you were to subtract sexual fantasy from the sum of human behaviour, what would happen to the population curve? For it struck him that thinking about breasts and bums and deep, vertical belly-buttons, and all that, was allowable, had always gone on, was indeed necessary to humanity, without its necessarily deviating into vice. And anyway, was there even such a thing as vice? Was Hitler a sinner? May not Hitler too be among the redeemed? His thinking began to wobble when he got to this point.

What about the impulse to procreate? He had married out of three modes of love. He had begun by wanting *to be married*, to have the game over with on favourable terms. He had wanted to become a father, making the customary valuable contribution to the existence of another generation. He had succeeded in this, Gary and Irene supplying proof of the satisfied desire. And he had longed to fuck Viv, and still wanted to fuck her. The first time he'd seen her he had imagined her in bed with him naked, ready for union. He still couldn't contemplate a life without sexual longing. He still wanted to fuck Viv, and had stayed with her for thirty years, and now feminist theoretics seemed to undermine his sexy *rationale*.

Was no sexual stimulus decent and lawful, or were all? One of his favourite movies of all time – or at least all time up to now – was the wonderful English farce *The Green Man*, with its admirable cast, Alastair Sim, Terry-Thomas, George Cole, and best of all the splendid Jill Adams. Lovely, adorable Jill Adams, by far the most beautiful of the Monroe *seguaci*, much more lovely than even Marilyn herself, though cursed by the fact that she had come after rather than before the famed sexpot. There's nothing to be had out of doing something second; it's desperately important to be the original, not the carbon. Jill Adams never managed to get out from under the hard circumstances of being the second young woman in the mid-1950s to come across like that on the screen. She really was lovelier than Marilyn but it was MM who got the fame and the sad fortune. Jill Adams, highly intelligent, immensely sweet, with her breathless voice and her charming floating feather-cut blond tresses, and her full-breasted, slender-waisted torso and her pouting lips, enjoyed a shortish career in British farces and a long obscurity after 1965.

In the fifties in *The Green Man*, Bronson had always remembered with longing and affection, there were two entrancing leisurely sequences in which lovely Jill retired to her bedroom and there, alone before a large vanity mirror, modelled one of those sensational black corsets or waist-cinchers that you never see any more, the kind that lifted the breasts and exposed their upper surfaces, at the same time nipping in the lovely waist and rounding and projecting the buttocks in a smooth glacis offering slight resistance to armed approach. The action depicted in these sequences had absolutely no causal link to the rest of the absurd story. It had been thrown in as incidental enticement and yet – this was certainly peculiar – the corset sequences had a most peculiar air of innocence and delicate charm; there was nothing in the least salacious or pornographic about them. Bronson could never quite understand how this had been managed, for in principle this unabashed exhibition of a woman's body should have exhaled a noisome indelicacy from which decent men and women would instinctively recoil. But it didn't.

How did *The Green Man* get around the pitfall of indecency? Was it the perfect idiocy of the story which redeemed it from any connection with real passion or lust? Was it the unconcealed delight with which pretty Jill appeared on the set in her captivating underwear? We never see her naked. Both sequences start with the girl securely clasped in the embrace of her elaborate underclothing. Was it the actress's grace and beauty and plain enjoyment of her role? Was it simply that the British have excelled in sex farce for a century and do it better than anybody else? It's impossible to say, but Bronson understood, as he meditated over the intense pleasure offered by the two questionable sequences, that somehow or other *The Green Man* remained an unutterably charming entertainment and that Jill Adams was blamelessly adorable. He wished he could have known her in the old days ... or even now. Could there be a film library somewhere housing British comedies of the fifties that could be borrowed for longer or shorter periods for home study? What a useful facility that would be!

And then one Christmas Viv, and Gary and Irene, who were grown up and living in distant places, collaborated on his present, something he'd never dreamed of acquiring for himself, a high-quality, state-of-the-tech VCR that could perform a thousand mysterious operations, always supposing that its master or mistress could decipher the instruction manual, which was written in a peculiar English corroded by acronyms and accompanied by little arrows indicating critical operational paths. These instructions at first baffled and then angered Bronson. He has never yet, after the passage of considerable time, succeeded in actually taping a programme while absent from the house. Nor has he managed to set the contrivance to come on while he's asleep, or to come on while he's going to bed, thereafter turning itself off. He has trouble setting the clock. The stop and search mode continues to confound him. He just rolls the tape on past the beginning of whatever it is he wants to see on the cassette, then rewinds, then fast-forwards, gradually narrowing down the gap – he's getting quite good at this –

until he's at the final frames of whatever it is that precedes the opening titles of the material he wants to show.

But what the hell, he's managed to master the two or three basic modes of VCR operation. He can tape televised material. He can even tape while watching something else, a skill he's intensely proud of. He can sooner or later find the beginning of something he wants to rerun. He can interrupt a rerun by going to the pause mode and can edit out commercials while taping new films by going to the same mode and watching the little white lines shrink across the screen; he can eliminate the 'this film not to be copied' announcement. He can get into frame-by-frame, which allows highly concentrated inspection of individual frames of films in a way never previously available to ordinary people who like movies but aren't professional film cutters or editors.

It was quite a while after New Year's, following weeks and weeks of fumbling with the buttons on the remote control unit, figuring out the distinction between rewind-after-stop and simple rewind-while-showing, and other sophisticated matters, that Bronson fully grasped the more recherché uses of his Christmas gift. You could stop a taped movie at any point, then make it flip onward very very slowly a frame at a time, allowing extremely close attention to details of the set-dressing, say, or the continuity. What kind of car was Dan Duryea driving in *Lady on a Train?* How exactly did the staircase fit into the centre of the house in *The Spiral Staircase?* Things like that. Close inspection of the state of dress or undress of attractive young women was not quite the first use of these powers that presented itself to him.

But a little while after his first flush of investigative enthusiasm it struck him that you could get a really good look at what women were wearing, simply by stopping the tape and then moving it forward a frame at a time. This realization came to him in a blinding flash when he read in the weekend TV guide that his local PBS outlet was about to hold a two-week British comedy film festival. The Boultings, Launder and Gilliatt, the early Ealings. Films to be shown included three of the *Carry On* series, a couple of Alec Guinness classics, and a sextet of other fifties charmers. *Carleton-*

Browne of the F.O., *Brothers-in-Law, I'm All Right, Jack, Two-Way Stretch, Belles of Saint Trinian's,* and Hallelujah, *The Green Man.*

Were those underwear shots really in the film or had he simply imagined them over thirty years and elaborated them in fevered reconstruction? Was Jill Adams as fetching and as worthy of super-star status (if it hadn't been for poor old Marilyn) as his acute criti-cal faculty insistently suggested? Friday night at eleven he was on the edge of his recliner in front of the screen and the VCR, remote control clutched convulsively in the left hand, fingers of the right hand at the ready as the announcer declared that tonight's British comedy festival feature was the Alastair Sim/George Cole vehicle *The Green Man.* On came the cute titles and the silly music and in the opening frames Alastair Sim unveiled for the audience his career as maker of infernal machines and political assassin. The film then went on its hilarious way at breakneck speed to the point where George Cole meets Jill Adams in the cosy little house in Turnham Green in which she is about to settle down to married life with her fiancé, an insufferable BBC type.

The audience sees at once that George and Jill are going to get together in the end; maybe the two corset-in-front-of-the-vanity incidents are in the picture to emphasize what a happy ending this will be, the union of two loving young hearts in a shining psycho-logical and sexual consummation. Everybody loves that happy ending; it is in the terms of Northrop Frye the classical argument of comedy. Bronson certainly bought it a hundred percent.

When he'd finished making his tape he quite literally hugged himself. He wound his skinny arms around his torso ecstatically and went on his way to bed telling himself that now he had a tape of *The Green Man* which he could consult whenever he liked. At first he wasn't perfectly clear which parts of the film were to be the objects of study. But Monday night found him gazing intently at the screen, fondling his remote-control unit. He fast-forwarded his cassette until he got to the place where Jill tells George that she expects to find him gone – and her hearthrug immaculate – when she comes downstairs. She goes to her bedroom carrying an armful of parcels. Cut to medium-shot, interior, day, the bedroom. Jill is standing in front of her big mirror fastening a final garter to a stocking and admiring her undeniably sensational appearance in this extremely sexy piece of black underwear. The film retains and even intensifies its effect of charming innocence. The audience feels very much on darling Jill's side. She's modelling this new bit of lingerie to gauge the effect it will have on her husband-to-be, maybe on their honeymoon or on their first night together in this very bedroom. She succeeds in making the audience feel really happy and pleased for her in a way that Marilyn Monroe could never have managed, poor doomed creature.

And at one moment in the first sequence she attains a pitch of sensuous intensity never achieved by any exhibition of Marilyn's beauty. Jill turns this way and that in front of her mirror, adjusts her bra cups, tugs an edging of lace down behind, and then, hearing footsteps outside the bedroom door, she gives a start of alarm and turns towards the camera in comic bewilderment, bending forward involuntarily and raising a creamy arm in a gesture of defiance. When she leans forward her nipples, and the huge, very stirring, dark circles around them are momentarily visible – certainly for less than a second. Such a brief moment in fact that ordinary viewers with ordinary vision can't spot them. Neither do the censors. The moment has never been cut from the prints in use on TV.

In his experimenting with the remote control, Bronson approached these crucial frames very gingerly, using the frame-by-frame mode. When he got to this point in the film he nearly expired from sudden excess of joy. He'd never seen anything like it. If twenty-four frames were being exposed per second (or whatever the correct speed is), Jill's nipples were visible for about two-fifths of a second, or about eleven frames. He accessed the stop-action mode at about the fifth frame and gazed and gazed at a tiny segment of life captured thirty-four years earlier and stilled into eternity. There they were. They would be gone before another second began. Gather me, he thought, into the artifice of the temporal. Such is life, so brief, so eventful and so dependent on the relative speed or slowness of our sensory reactions. The plump perky nubbins, the superb curve of breast rising about them, most arousing of all the dark, profoundly womanly, shadowy areola, lurking forever under their sheath of clothing, were revealed achingly briefly. He flipped to the sixth frame, the seventh, onwards to the point where the actress recovered her balance and began to straighten up, so that the angle of the shot altered enough to cover her nakedness. It might be, in the age before the VCR, that even the original living Jill never knew how much of herself she had exposed in those two-fifths of a second. Bronson sat there entranced. He felt that this experience clarified for him yet another of the benefits of free liberal democracy in a technological age. Fifty years before, only top film stars and big producers had enjoyed private projection. Frame-by-frame study was practicable only by cutters and editors in the studios. Today anybody with a VCR could approach movies in a professional way, the mysteries of the form being unveiled before anybody who cared enough to look. Democracy in action, thought Bronson.

He rewound the tape and prepared to pass the first and better of the two sequences through frame-by-frame inspection for a second time. He expected to be doing a lot of this from now on, but in his enthusiasm, perhaps in a moment of what the Greeks called *hubris,* or perhaps only because he still had not mastered all the subtleties of his VCR, he omitted to nip off that small black plastic square that prevents accidental erasure of material on the cassette. He reached the first Jill-in-corset shot, went to frame-by-frame and started to watch for the nipples revealed. He kept his finger on the right button ... one more frame ... another....

Behind him there came a slapping noise, feet crossing bare floor. His wife's voice said, 'Why, you dirty thing!'

Bronson's finger leaped involuntarily off the surface of the remote-control unit. Then without knowing what he was doing he pressed REC instead of PAUSE. Before he could react he'd obliterated thirty seconds of *The Green Man.* He cried out in agonized apprehension and rewound the cassette to the place where George Cole is creeping along the hall toward the bedroom. Then he was into the corset shot and all of a sudden there was snow on the screen and then an interview in colour with two women in their sixties, clad in outdoorswomen's gear, about to erect a tent on a camping trip in northern Vermont. Then there was more snow, and then a strange unrolling-from-the-top-down effect. The sound of the film came back on, a shadowy picture swam out of nowhere and here came Jill, striding along the upstairs hall, then descending the staircase in a voluminous black negligée of the most chaste *couture*. Bronson goggled.

Behind him, Viv's voice ejaculated, 'Oh, what have I done?'

'Aaaaaagggghhhhh,' said Bronson.

'Oh, honey, don't, please,' said Viv. 'It was an accident. Run it back. Maybe some of it's left. Maybe the campers are just superimposed....'

He rewound and fast-forwarded desperately but the nipples were gone.

'It'll be on again sometime,' said Viv imploringly. 'We'll write to channel 33. We'll bombard them with requests under assumed names. We might even pledge a monthly contribution during the next fund-raising drive if they agree to meet our conditions.'

Her husband slowly recovered the cassette from the bowels of the VCR and flicked the little plastic protective square across the room with his thumbnail.

'That's what that's for,' he said.

'It'll be on again.'

'I pressed the wrong button.'

'You poor lamb. Come on, let's go up.'

She put her arm entreatingly around his waist and together they mounted to their bedroom. Maybe the pornographic impulse had its uses after all.

Now, every Saturday morning Bronson and Viv tear the *Gazette* apart like a pair of rampant young lions, looking for the weekly TV guide, scanning it together in one another's arms, hoping for a rerun of *The Green Man.*

Don't Bother Coming

WELL, IT'S A LONG STORY and it isn't over. Picture the Adirondacks just after the war, along the lonely highway between Plattsburgh and Camp Drum, the northern tier, country almost empty. Back behind Au Sable Forks, Lake Placid, Saranac with a scanty population living on the proceeds of bumper-stickers. Winter Sports Capital of the USA. Land of Make Believe. Mount Marcy: Highest Point in New York. Santa's Workshop. Mount Pisgah. Seasonal, very seasonal. An integral part of New York State (at that epoch the most populous state in the union) and as desolate a region as any in Canada. The regional metropolis was Montréal.

The Lippards and the Gracies lived in there, sprinkled along the stretch between Tupper Lake and Cranberry Lake, earning a modest living from the geography. The Gracies were the old aboriginal family of the district, who made a good thing out of constructing lakeside camps and cabins or doing some guiding or perhaps operating a lost little gas station and general store. You'd see the name Gracie on RFD boxes and storefronts for fifty miles along the road. The Lippards weren't native Adirondack people. Mr Lippard was a civil engineer, a civilian who worked on construction at Camp Drum at a time when some very mysterious work was going on there, just before and during the war. A close-mouthed and buttoned-up man by nature, he met Mona Gracie at a mixer in Fargo and married her as silently and inscrutably as he did most other things. The marriage was – perhaps as a consequence – appallingly serene. Sam Lippard would be shrouded in military secrecy fifty miles off while family affairs along the roadside in the mountains unfolded in their dreamy way. Young Danny Lippard attended what must have been the smallest high school in New York State, maybe in the entire U.S., where his mother's sister, Aunt Alice Gracie, was pretty nearly the entire English department. Tupper Lake H.S., where from season to season Coach Boutsma couldn't muster more than the absolute bare minimum of warm bodies necessary to field a losing football squad. No able-bodied male adolescent could be allowed not to go out for football, no matter how unqualified he might be by reason of natural ineptitude. A strange football team: the Tupper Lake Mountaineers. We used to bus the squad twenty-five or forty miles downhill to Carthage or Gouverneur and they never won a game, not in a decade.

Dan's older sisters Terry-Jane and Babs were the cheerleaders – the only cheerleaders – for the whole time of their high school attendance and for a year or two of cartwheels after graduation. Dan himself played safety most of the time, with an occasional turn on offence at wide receiver. He had no talent at all for pass receptions, absolutely none, but a fair turn of speed downfield. He very infrequently caught a pass but never scored.

He didn't mind playing football; it was a dirty business but somebody had to do it. What he really liked was sitting around talking to his Aunt Alice about nothing in particular, sometimes for three hours through a winter evening, in the living room of her small snug house, really a winterized summer cabin, half a mile up a dirt track from the highway. Many nights through the late fall and winter the lights of Alice's place were all you saw, coming up the track from the crumbling blacktop. Just the few little lights and the shadowy small mass of the building. For some obscure reason Alice got the best TV reception in the hills and used to invite the Gracies and Lippards over for the principal TV events of the season. Dan was about the only person who ever paid much attention to her invitations. He got his basic notions about what women are like through this friendship with his aunt, the closest tie of his life.

At any time in this century up to the early nineteen-sixties women like Alice Gracie could find a dignified place in most social situations, as single women, unmarried aunts, maiden ladies, spinsters, even as old maids. The tone of these phrases varied from neutral, *single women, unmarried aunts,* through indulgent, *maiden ladies,* to comically dismissive, *spinsters, old maids.* What is a spinster anyway, besides a woman who has remained single? Somebody who has gone on spinning in solitude? 'They toil not, neither do they spin,' was spoken of the lilies of the field. A spinster certainly wasn't one of those. Originally the word meant simply, 'one who spins,' that is, a person who produces yarn from raw wool, someone proficient in the manufacture of needed textiles, often homespun. It was a word which might be applied indifferently to men and women, like the surnames Cardwell and Weaver and Webster. But more women than men passed their lives at the spinning-wheel. Sex wasn't indicated by the suffix of the term; a woman spinster wasn't a *spinstress*. She might be an actress, an anchoress, a poetess, but would remain a spinster. Difference of sex takes us in different ways. On the whole we thought of spinsters with humour and qualified pride when we were younger. Alice Gracie might have been described by her friends with a smile and an almost admiring description of her oddities at the time when she was young Dan Lippard's good buddy.

'I don't know what this community would do without her.' This was in 1950 when she ran the United Fund Campaign for the first time, more than doubling the previous year's contributions.

'Everybody in the county learned their punctuation from Alice,' said by the local postmistress in 1957 while looking over a pile of newly-sorted outgoing mail. 'She is one stickler for capital letters where they belong.'

'Alice got the brains,' said succinctly and quietly by Sam Lippard, several times during World War II, often in the nineteen-fifties, and once or twice as late as 1965, when women in her position were being marked down as somehow retarded or half-formed as though to be an unmarried aunt, a single woman, was disgraceful, almost perverse. By then, as we remember, a half-baked and muddled – even addled – Freudianism had invaded our minds, proposing sexual dysfunction as the motive for all behaviour which did not conform to a tiresome norm. It was considered usual, customary, proper, for women to seek their fulfilment in marriage and family life from 1955 through 1970. Women who stayed single were frankly a little oddball unless they were already well into middle age, in which case they might be excused for not having known any better, for having conducted their lives as though an unmarried woman were not best thrown on the dunghill the moment she reached thirty.

'A vocation to the single life.' Hoary traditional phrase with disagreeable Christian overtones and undertones. Made us think of *nuns*. Who could possibly be called to an asexual life? Or was it after all an asexual life? Wasn't it invariably a screen for covert and frustrated longing? Sure. That was it! All those people, bachelors, spinsters, were just covering up something. The men were gay, or funny uncles who liked to plant baby daughter on their knees and do ostensibly decent but secretly corrupt things to her. And the women were worse. Who could tell what went on in *convents*, for God's sakes. All right, so they'd gotten rid of those fifteenth-century costumes, what did that prove? They were still nothing but a half-nutty bunch of frustrated old maids.

The voice of the mid-sixties.

And hey, what did that voice know? Twenty years later it sounds as thoughtless, stupid, uncaring, ill-informed as it was at the time, and the nuns and Aunt Alice come up smelling – you should pardon the expression – like roses.

For they were the models of today's independent powerful wise women who are increasingly directing our lives; yesterday's old maid is today's feminist empress. It now appears that certain women can get along just fine, thanks, without a husband or another man of their own age in tow. Alice Gracie thought that her nephew Dan was the decentest and most intelligent person in Tupper Lake; she welcomed him into her small home for that reason. She took ninety evenings, seated in front of her TV watching *Playhouse 90* and *Hallmark Hall of Fame* productions, to knit Dan the most beautiful woollen team sweater in the form of a cardigan, bright buttons down the front, puffy flocked team letter over the left breast, in the Mountaineers' colours, crimson and gold. He was the only player on the team to have such a royal garment. After Alice gave it to him quite casually one November night – not as an early Christmas gift, not as a reward for good grades, not in the least as a hint at concealed passions – all the other players wanted one and couldn't get one. Alice had contrived the pattern for herself, and refused to circulate it.

The aunt and nephew used to exchange critical commentaries on what they saw on TV, often live productions of a quality not to be matched at the present time. 'Requiem for a Heavyweight,' 'Little Moon of Alban,' 'Twelve Angry Men,' 'Marty,' Peter Ustinov's touching impersonation of Doctor Johnson, dozens of late night re-runs of thirties movies in black and white, now rarely seen on the box. 'I am a Fugitive from a Chain Gang,' 'Little Caesar,' 'The Petrified Forest'. Television wasn't invariably a dreary wasteland in the fifties. In places like Tupper Lake a pair of friends could pass two or three hours on a Thursday or Friday evening looking at the network programming without feelings of alienated contempt. Dan acquired his earliest understanding of the nature of art by listening to his aunt's shrewd comments on acting and direction as elicited by what they saw on the screen. There was no other person in the region who might have offered such a commentary. Contact with art through television, and commercially sponsored television at that! What an absurd dream! And yet in the case of a very few people this miracle actually came to pass. Alice and Dan would sit side by side on the sagging sofa, passing a sack of potato chips back and forth, exchanging canny comments on production values, as some obscure film from the depths of the Depression years unfolded before them at midnight on Friday – no school on Saturday.

'Warner Brothers, the studio with a social conscience,' Alice would say. And a mysterious vague whiff of contests and torments enacted in almost unimaginably remote places and times would drift into the couple's shared experience, stuff which nobody in the five hundred square miles around them was equipped to understand.

She had books on architecture which she showed him, coffee-table-sized books, outsized folios they seemed to Danny, great floppy things. He particularly liked one which was devoted to the buildings of the great public expositions of the last century, in London and Paris and Vienna and Chicago and Saint Louis – the last a twentieth-century example of the genre, though a very early one. Alice would hum:

'Meet me in Saint Louis, Louis,
Meet me at the fair....'

Dan forever afterwards associated the pleasant little tune with an enormous two-page rendering of the Crystal Palace in steel engraving, showing the extraordinary characteristics of its construction. Looking through these books together they would turn and gaze silently into each other's faces with a dreadfully enjoyable sense of complicity.

Once towards the end of his high school days Aunt Alice passed on to him some tattered copies of *The Kenyon Review,* a journal written in a lexicon that Danny found simply incomprehensible. He had had no idea that there were living people who wrote in those terms. What were they trying to get at? And who were the strange publishers advertised in those conservatively-printed pages? Henry Regnery, New Directions, Bollingen Books, Schocken Books. Watching her nephew wrinkle his forehead over the magazines, Alice might divulge the title of the next play to be attempted by the high school dramatic society, *The Masquers.*

'I'm thinking of a courtroom drama for this season. What do you think of the idea? Trial scenes are surefire.'

'You don't want me to be in it?' Dan never decided how to address his aunt in those days. He couldn't quite call her by her first name and 'Aunt' or 'Auntie' was out of the question. He usually settled for no name at all, accompanied by a tentative smile.

'Dan, you have no talent whatsoever for acting, but you could handle most of the stage carpentry. The flats you built for "Miss Personality Plus" haven't warped at all. We'll repaint them for this year's set. Have you ever read "The Night of January 16th"?'

'No.'

'Take this home with you.' She handed him a stiff new acting copy of the play. 'Next time tell me what you think.'

That was the practical beginning of Dan's work with building and design. 'The Night of January 16th' contains a series of plot-twists which make necessary certain peculiarities in the set-design. Alice and Dan worked out a simple but effective revolving platform which allowed surprise effects that stunned the audience. Tupper Lake was agog; people who saw the play on the first or second night actually refused to divulge to their friends what was going to happen.

'No no, just wait and see. You'll be thrilled.'

There are still a few members of those original audiences alive, proud parents who recall their children's appearances in that play getting on for forty years ago. With a background like this it was natural for Dan to choose civil engineering as his career goal. He was accepted into the programme at McGill at the end of the fifties, when permanent passage back and forth across the Canadian/US border was easier to accomplish than it is today. After two years in civil, he decided to transfer to architecture and was able to get into the School of Architecture at the University of Toronto. He graduated in 1967 when excitement about architecture was at a high pitch in Canada.

He joined a Montréal partnership which was gradually feeling its way into an expert knowledge of the use of pre-stressed concrete in extremely cold weather situations. A few years later the firm received a series of sub-contracts and consultancies in connection with the construction of the Olympic Stadium in Montréal. Dan's work on the fitting of the various prefabricated concrete pieces in the upper rim of the huge structure, carried out against an onrushing deadline in the face of grave miscalculations in the designs, won him the kind of celebrity that a rising professional may achieve among his peers while remaining in total obscurity as far as the great public is concerned. There were trips to Israel and Japan, more recently a consultative position on the designs for the National Gallery in Ottawa. Dan's life turned further and further away from its beginnings. Family and friends found lodging at the extreme back of his thoughts. He could almost be said to have forgotten all of them. He married. He and his wife enjoyed parenthood very much. Soon the children were assuming personalities.

Definite surprising identities of their own. The federal government accepted the Safdie proposals for the National Gallery. Suddenly Dan had a commission – not for the partnership, specifically his own – for a fascinating housing project in New Delhi. It struck him at this busy time towards the end of the seventies that his affections and energies were all being directed into his professional life. His wife now gave most of her attention to the children, a boy and a girl so distinct in their identities as almost to be strangers to him. And over beyond them – on their other side, so to speak – his wife nurtured them and presided over their approach to adolescence. He never saw his parents any more, although Tupper Lake was only a two-hour drive from Montréal, say two and a half in winter weather. Alice Gracie was finally not much more than a shadow in his surface imagination, a persistent obscure presence, the person who had early in his life shown him the big picture of the Great Exhibition and told him what the Crystal Palace was and who had put it in place. Dan made two fairly long trips to New Delhi at this period; he felt that he was growing away from his education into world citizenship....

The telephone rang sharply about seven o'clock on a wintry Friday night in 1980. Young Sandy took the call, listened to the speaker with a puzzled expression on his face, then spoke to his father who was downstairs in his workroom looking through some floor plans.

'For you, Dad.'

'Who is it?'

'I think it's grandma.'

Dan picked up the phone in his workroom with reluctance; he felt that he had really arrived at middle-age when he realized how much he hated answering the phone. He gave his name guardedly. The caller, a woman, began to speak hastily, her words tumbling over one another in her unusual state of emotion. Of course, the caller was his mom.

'Oh, Dan, Dan. I'm so glad I caught you in. I should have called earlier but I thought maybe you were still in India, I didn't know for sure.'

'What's the matter?'

'It's Alice, Dan.'

He had to think for a moment to bring the name into focus. 'Alice?'

'Your Aunt Alice, my big sister, you remember. Well, for goodness' sake, you ought to remember if anybody does; you always used to be up at her place. She's had a stroke, Dan, and she isn't expected to last very long. I shouldn't have bothered you but I thought perhaps you'd like to know.'

'I'll come right down,' he said without knowing why.

'Oh, no, Danny dear, you needn't do that. It isn't like you were that close any more, and you can't do anything really. Don't bother coming; it would simply be a waste of time. I only called because I feel bad about Alice. It must have been hours before anybody found her and she isn't ... well, she isn't ... I don't know, I was always just the baby sister.'

'I should be there before midnight,' he said.

He didn't know why he'd said that. There had been snow earlier in the day; it might still be snowing in the hills. The highway. That highway, God! He hadn't driven in from Plattsburgh for – how long was it, a decade? He was very used to travel and knew just what to stow in a light overnight bag. 'I don't know just when I'll be back,' he told his wife. 'I'll call you from the hospital. It shouldn't be more than a day or so.' He didn't anticipate any involvement in the death of an aging relative whom he knew virtually nothing about. His mother's older sister, the high school English teacher. They used to read poetry together. He remembered this with a certain uneasiness as he crossed the Champlain Bridge about eight-fifteen and settled down for the easy ride to Plattsburgh. It was cold outside, you could tell from the way the snow hung heavy and still on the dark forms of trees. A few lights burned in the distance on either side of the highway. He considered smoking, then rejected the notion. The smoke fouled the atmosphere in the car and anyway he seemed to be growing out of the need to smoke. The car behaved beautifully; there were no traffic problems. He turned onto the back highway about nine-twenty.

All at once the name and the powerful visage of Sir Joseph Paxton drifted into his mind, and then a clear picture of the transept of the Crystal Palace: entryway of wrought iron presided over by a Yeoman of the Guard, fine trees twining up under the great glass barrel-vaulting. And then a richly detailed rendering of the huge structure as seen from the northwest. 'In the right foreground is the steam-engine house.' He remembered all that, and it had been his aunt who first showed it to him. He began to realize, as he drove along the rising slopes into the forest that he was who he was because of his early friendship with this dying woman who occupied such a tiny corner of his consciousness, a shard of memory. He drove directly to the small Tupper Lake Hospital, arriving about eleven-thirty. There was plenty of parking and there seemed to be hardly anybody around. He spotted his parents' car, an unpretentious Oldsmobile.

A night nurse drowsed in a revolving chair next to the information desk. He cleared his throat softly once or twice and she straightened up and directed him to the private ward on the second floor. The building was very new, solidly framed in and extremely quiet; the floor tiling absorbed the sound of his footsteps, which seemed to come from a long way off as though they were on the soundtrack of a movie. One or two people, Terry-Jane and her hubby, Dan's mom, a youngish doctor, were grouped outside his aunt's room. They filled him in quickly on the state of the case, the doctor disposing of Aunt Alice's chances with professional objectivity. 'Another twelve to eighteen hours, then the terminal insult.' He had other cases to attend to, decent well-intentioned man. He gave his opinion with modest forthrightness and moved away in the direction of more hopeful undertakings. Dan's sister and his mother faced him tremulously. They were sorry, they declared, to have brought him all this way. How was his wife, how were the children?

'I'll go in now,' he said. 'Is there anybody with her?'

'There's us. Do you want us to come in with you?'

'It doesn't matter. Come if you want to.' He opened the heavy quiet door and went into the room. A solid, strangely reassuring,

maple office chair was positioned at the bedside. He settled himself
into it and looked down at the motionless figure on the bed. He'd
expected to find a tangle of medical apparatus, tubes and bottles
and the equipment for reading brain impulses, but there was nothing there. She must be past that, he thought, and he leaned to his
left, bending forward and sideways in his chair, and with some mis-
givings took up his aunt's left hand. She didn't seem to be breathing
but she must have been, because the hand, while cold and inert,
seemed to be faintly animated by a very slow pulse. He didn't know
what to say or how to address her. He'd never used her Christian
name before. They had belonged to different generations and it
would have been an impertinence. But he called her by name now.

'Alice,' he said, clearly and softly. 'Alice.' Nothing happened.

He took the cold hand in both his palms and stroked it gently.

'Alice, it's me. It's Dan. It's Danny.' He began to talk quietly to
her about the Crystal Palace and the realization of his own ambi-
tions. 'The impression of almost limitless space,' he heard himself
say, 'was enhanced by the colour-scheme devised by Owen Jones,
which was based on his belief that in all great periods of art only the
primary colours were used. Blue was the predominant colour, and
was used on the columns and girders. This must have given a misty
appearance to the interior.'

To his very great astonishment, he felt his aunt's hand begin to
grow warm, the faint impression of a pulse to grow more distinct.

'Touches of yellow gave variety,' he said falteringly.

Alice opened her eyes and looked directly at him. 'And bold
expanses of red,' she whispered, 'behind the balconies and as a
backdrop for the exhibits, provided bright accents.'

'It's me, Alice it's Dan.' Her hand grew warmer still and stirred
in his grasp. 'It is *I*,' she said with a mild emphasis. 'Of course it's
Dan. Who else would it be?'

'Mom and Terry-Jane have been here right along,' he said, 'and I
came as soon as I heard.'

'Well, you've done me good,' said Alice positively. 'How do I
arrange to leave the hospital? We are in the hospital, aren't we?'

'That's correct.'

'How long have I been here?' She couldn't believe it when they told her. 'I was just cutting up some potatoes for fries when I felt dizzy. Was that Monday?'

She had been comatose for most of four days. During the discussion she seemed to gain strength, some very peculiar access of renewed vitality which was never afterwards adequately explained. Various doctors keep asking her why she responded to her nephew. What did she hear when he spoke? What did she recognize? Was it the familiar hand, just the right voice? Why him in particular? Nobody has been able to figure this out. It was all a long time ago anyway and she has other things to think about. Today at eighty she's planning her trip to New Delhi with Dan's mom, just to see what he's been getting up to lately.

Hot Cockatoos

EDGAR MILLSAPS, a parrot fancier who simply could not get enough of these colourful winged companions, from earnest collecting at unmanageable expense at last descended to theft. We know that collectors generally possess the psychology of thieves. Many are the unedifying tales told of medal or book collectors, for example, of the substitution of ingenious forgeries for true first folios, of the false naming of medals from the Crimean War to survivors of the charge of the Light Brigade. These and other instances, mysterious disappearances of smallish easel paintings from galleries, or of eighteenth-century cow creamers from glass cases in obscure country houses, may be multiplied to support the view that for 'collector' we must often write 'thief'.

Long since left to himself by wife and deeply embarrassed children, Millsaps had continued to dwell in a mid-Ontario city home with an extensive, screened-in bird run sited in his gardens, until he and his cherished pets were driven by the curses and threats of neighbours into resentment-tainted exile in an unspecified wilderness place. Country residence seemed dictated by pending court proceedings and several nighttime attempts to free his birds by punching holes in the (lightly electrified) screening. Debate over the landlord's presumptive right to hedge his property by electrification (as in precedents of farmer and cattle) seemed about to issue at County Court level in the laying of charges including the phrase 'intent to cause bodily harm.' Millsaps, very rich but not endowed with bottomless pockets, may have decided that even his great fortune did not constitute an adequate shield against the depredations of those who seek malicious recourse to law in civil or worse, in criminal proceedings.

In *Atwood vs. Millsaps, 35 Eliz.* II, CC *Lennox and Addington*, we find the relevant legal documentation. Plaintiff alleges civil responsibility for injuries sustained while freeing bird on humanitarian grounds. Defendant proposes counter-suit seeking damages for loss of valuable specimen lorikeet, breakage, injury to reputation, headaches and nervous complaints consequent upon felonious conduct of neighbour. Decision reserved.

One of the fleet of magnificent macaws ranged in an area of the run adjacent to the lorikeets' quarters, his attention attracted by the unusual behaviour of complainant, had managed to work his beak through the loose weave of the wiring at a crucial place, and from this stance had inflicted a cruel flesh-wound upon Atwood bending. The facts came out in court; telling photographs of the contusion – in brilliant colour – were produced before the inspecting eye of justice. The case seemed likely to go against defendant. It was at this epoch that the obsessed ornithologist and his flock quitted suburban Beechwood Manor overnight and were not seen there again.

Rumours circulated in the mid-Ontario city of macaws and Patagonian conures – those shrieking generations – silenced that night by stun-guns and surreptitious injections. Animal Rights activists and Humane Society officials would have liked to learn the subsequent whereabouts of the Millsaps' collection. A small squadron of unmarked panel trucks painted in inconspicuous blues and greys had appeared in the centre of Beechwood Manor on a murmurous summer night. All at once the cries and flappings of the Millsaps' birds were stilled. Indistinct shapes went back and forth between screening and panelled compartments. Then the procession moved silently away and at dawn the aviary was seen to have been disembarrassed of birdlife. The inconsequence and shortsightedness of humankind being what they are, some Beechwood Manorites soon began to assert that they rather missed the birds after all....

The skies of mid-Ontario were cleared of alien wings; the small city and suburb went untroubled by the disharmonious sounding-together (symphony) of nighttime outcries, formerly valued by Mr Millsaps as an effective burglar alarm. Never in his tenure of the Beechwood Manor estate had his home been broken into by criminals or vandals, who were frightened of the noises. If you've ever entered a bird sanctuary or listened to a formation of southbound

Canada geese on Thanksgiving weekend, you'll understand how minor criminals felt about Edgar Millsaps and his parrot friends. And it is probably good that the criminal classes be now and then put in fear by another social agency than the police. In Beechwood Manor the criminal classes were scared shitless of parrots. In casting away from ourselves some mixed blessing, we often open the door to unmixed affliction. When petty crime began to increase sharply in Beechwood Manor immediately after Millsaps took an inconspicuous leave, some suburbanites mourned what they had given up, and wished they had it back. The birds had not been such a nuisance as that. One could not have wished to live right next door to them but all the same....

There followed a period of adjustment to the new aerial reality. Now and then a sighting of exotic and highly-coloured bird life drew coverage in the suburban newspaper.

BLUEBIRD NO LONGER ENDANGERED SPECIES
Starling invasion quelled; famed North
American species reasserts nesting right.

Those of us who hadn't actually observed the new bluebirds, secretly and sometimes even openly proposed that this exotic blue creature now fairly frequently sighted was not the old Eastern Bluebird at all, but simply some dowdy parrot or other that had effected an escape during the notorious nighttime transmigration of Millsaps' collection which, according to skilled professionals, had numbered in the hundreds and perhaps thousands.

Whichever opinion you might hold, you had to realize that with the growing incidence of small unsolved breakings and enterings that now ensued in the region, there was as an accompanying parallel development some sort of mysterious disturbance in the lives of those who kept small birds as pets, and of those who catered professionally to their requirements, proprietors of pet-shops. A few zoos were involved too. The plain fact was that a lengthy series of very peculiar bird disappearances began about two months after Millsaps went away, at first with a couple of inexplicable vanishings of cockatoos, in one case a pair of the charming friendly creatures, of striking personality and high market value. These two birds, Ike and Mike ('they look alike') had belonged to a fashionable local hotel, where they had been enshrined in the lobby on behalf of Best Western for almost a decade. Ike and Mike had learned to pronounce the words 'Best Western' in stunningly clear and cultivated mid-Atlantic diction. The hotel chain had originally hoped to breed the pair, eventually establishing a line of descent which might sooner or later staff other lobbies across Canada.

Nobody ever succeeded in sexing either Ike or Mike. These gentle birds were remarkably reluctant to allow the necessary intimate handling – as who wouldn't be, after all – and neither ever produced an egg, fertilized or unfertilized. One slightly larger than the other, with a faint pinkish tinge to their underdown and creamy pale yellow flowing crests, they entertained patrons of the medium to high-priced upper-middle-level midtown hotel/motel complex for nine enchanted years, then vanished.

A pet-shop proprietor with outlets from Belleville to Cornwall in a chain of triple-a malls complained to the police about an outbreak of thievery which apparently defied explanation. The malls, adequately guarded by night, seemed proof against conventional criminal operations. But this was no conventional unimaginative mafioso undertaking. This was *art!* It was clearly the work of somebody in the grip of an ardent obsession whose fascination with the birds had worked his imaging power up to a high intense pitch of invention. After many months of thinking through the matter, the OPP began to theorize that somebody who was crazy about birds was at the bottom of the case.

Some provincial police officers laboured under the uneasy suspicion that the whole affair resembled something in the movies. They had all seen *Batman* and knew that a mastermind with a deeply felt and long nurtured grudge against society might go to any lengths to encompass his crazy aims.

'Well, and if *Batman*,' said one veteran officer, 'why not *Birdman?*'

'Yeah, guys, what about that?'

Grumbling perplexed chorus of male voices.

'No no no, you've got it all wrong. Batman is on the side of law and order, isn't he?'

'So?'

'So ... so would Birdman be ... wouldn't he?'

'That seems an unprofitable speculation and must remain matter for conjecture.'

There was never any question of the magical or supernatural about the outbreak of bird larceny. It was simply that the amount of planning and cunning expended on what would otherwise be unremarkable thefts, perhaps the work of small boys, seemed to indicate the presence of somebody rich enough to own and maintain a helicopter of sizeable proportions.

The OPP officers would arrive the next day and stand on the tarred and gravelled flat roof of the desecrated mall or publicly-maintained aviary, examining the traces left overnight by the burglars.

'They look like the talon scrapings of some enormous bird,' said one investigator slowly.

His companions gazed at him sourly.

'Hell they do,' said a more self-controlled officer, Corporal Ralph Cavan, Gananoque Detachment, OPP. 'Those are helicopter marks, that's what those are. See? Here's where he put down, and here ...' he traced the movement of the skids, 'here's were he stopped. Look, you can see how the rotor has blown the gravel into little ripples.'

The other officers allowed themselves to be persuaded. One of them, the senior official of the district, made up his mind about the matter on the spot. 'I'm putting you in charge of this investigation, Cavan,' he said. 'You're detached from routine duty as of this moment, and I want results. There's far too much of this sort of thing going on in our sector and it's got to stop instanter, do you hear me? There's nothing unusual about this case at all. It's that bugger Millsaps, that's who it is. He's just figuring on getting even with everybody for running him out of Beechwood Acres.'

'Beechwood Manor, sir.'

'Whatever ... it's an open and shut case. Now get on it right away!'

Corporal Cavan saluted smartly and they all went downstairs through the access door. Most of them went around to Pizza Hut for lunch.

Later in the afternoon Ralph Cavan drove back to OPP headquarters, Gananoque, revolving many matters in his mind. He set up a command post in what had been the officers' recreational lounge. There were some objections to this, but when he pointed out the opportunities for glory and career advancement promised as the reward for successful management of the operation, his brother officers gave up their opposition.

'It'll be a fast-breaking case,' said one constable, grunting as he helped to shift a pinball machine out of the way so they could plug in the computer bank.

'I don't know about that so much,' said Corporal Cavan. 'We've got a lot of input to sift through.' They were just barely able to squeeze the fax machine in beside the coffee-maker.

They fed their number into the circuitry and began to monitor message-inflow. Most of what came in the first night was pretty trivial stuff, owls crashing through windshields in the Rouyn-Noranda district, turkey buzzards sighted where no turkey buzzard should normally be. Eventually though, towards the end of August, a pattern of sightings began to emerge from the information input.

A fisherman from Charleston Lake called in at headquarters one afternoon with a handful of curious photographs and strange story. He'd been trolling at a leisurely pace down Eastern Water towards dusk on the previous evening. All at once he had spotted a pair of birds standing erect on a nearby shelf of painted rock. Fortunately he had had his camera in the boat and had been able to get some documentation in the uncertain light. He fanned out a sheaf of excellent shots on Corporal Cavan's desk. What they showed was the silhouette of an enormous, greyish-blue bird, very thin, almost arrogant in the easy authority of its stance, a great blue heron. Such a sighting was commonplace, the heron being familiar in the region. What was genuinely startling was the presence in the picture of a second bird, smaller than the blue heron but exhibiting the same relaxed composure, obviously on excellent terms with his companion. The smaller bird stood in an attitude which seemed to parody comically the magnificence of the great glorious blue fisher-bird. But the plumage was different. This bird, one eye cocked in the direction of the photographer, bore white, faintly pinkish feathers, and on its noble head there streamed forth the creamy crest of the cockatoo.

'What did they have to say for themselves?' demanded Corporal Cavan.

'The heron hollered at me, "Fraaannnkkkk," you know the way they do. He wasn't scared or nothing. I'm down that way in the boat most evenings after supper.'

'And the other one?'

'He looked at me and said, "Best Western".'

'Ike, by God,' said a constable.

'Then he said something that sounded like "double occupancy".'

'Or Mike,' said Corporal Cavan. He riffled through the colour photos searchingly; this was the first major sighting in the course of the investigation. The officers took the fisherman into command headquarters and got him to point out on the map – an enormous blowup of linked aerial photographs of eastern Ontario – exactly where the sighting had occurred. He scanned the map with care, and after some hesitation placed a forefinger on a spot about one mile south of the mouth of Leeder's Creek. 'There,' he said, 'within one hundred feet or what is it now? Thirty metres?'

'A metre is around thirty-nine inches,' said Corporal Cavan.

'Well, say thirty-one metres,' said the fisherman.

They marked the sighting on the map with a red thumbtack and waited for further data so as to be able to triangulate. Meanwhile Ralph studied the terrain for several miles around the shore where the first sighting had occurred. Rocky, forested, up-and-down, empty, the highland on the east side of the lake was an opaque wilderness, reachable only by one of the virtually abandoned logging roads dating from the last century. This locality was in the same ecological situation as it had been long ago in the time of Christ.

'If he's in there, we'll never get him out,' thought Cavan, but he was not yet prepared to give up on the search. There seemed no possible way for Edgar Millsaps to have shipped his precious collection into the Blue Mountain area.

Cavan studied the map. No, he thought, he can't be in there. He's somewhere along one of the back roads. This perception – accurate enough in the event – didn't materially advance the investigation. The back country east of the lake is a terrible tangle of old deserted back roads, hundreds of miles of them no longer maintained by county or township, like the Dixie Road off Leeds County Road 5, or the old Webster Road near Lyndhurst. These tracks wind up into emptiness, abandoned barns and wagon sheds and fallen-in foundations becoming intermittent, infrequent, finally invisible. You can read what happened to the original settlers in the distribution of the buildings. The runaway collector/thief could be in hiding almost anywhere up one of these cowpaths.

'He's going in and out by helicopter. We've got to get more sightings,' concluded Corporal Cavan. The thefts from private homes and pet shops now increased in frequency. Budgies! Old women's cherished companions. Pairs of little lovebirds. Finches! Unimportant and nearly valueless birds. Arthur the famous mynah-bird of Stoverville. Was there no end to it?

A householder living at the intersection of the Eighth Concession Road and Highway 42 reported in with the corpse of a cockatiel found dead of exposure outside the toolshed at the back of his property. The sight of the stiffened small body angered Cavan; he swore to carry the case through to a finish. 'He's getting greedy,' he thought. 'Those cockatiels are the sweetest little things; that's some child's pet, I'll bet anything, and died from the overnight chill.' This was in the third week of September when a freak early frost had taken Leeds County without warning. A dead canary was found in an Athens backyard, and duly plotted on the big map. And then some enormous blue and red thing was spied circling and hovering like a hawk or eagle, high above Ballycanoe.

This was the fourth definite piece of information. When it was plotted on the map the investigators were sure they had something important to go on. The four sightings almost seemed to outline the limits of Millsap's airspace. Athens, Ballycanoe, the Eighth Concession Road, Eastern Water. Somewhere in the border area between Elizabethtown and Rear of Yonge and Escott. But where? All that country is going back to bush. There are dozens and perhaps hundreds of possible hiding-places in there, and only one or two means of access by car or van. As he studied the points on the grid and revolved the pattern of usable roadways in his head, Corporal Cavan all at once felt impelled to place his forefinger on a location towards which all his instincts directed him. He reached up and stabbed at the map. 'He's somewhere just about here,' he said. He saw that he had indicated a point on the Eighth Concession Road about two miles in from Highway 42, not far from the place where the overgrown back road crosses Wiltse Creek.

Like Napoleon or Lord Nelson, Corporal Cavan had always found it wise to follow his hunches. Who could guess what obscure, deeply concealed processes of intuition justified them? He stationed the two available OPP highway patrol vehicles at either end of this stretch of deserted back concession roadway, only recently paved and already starting to crumble at the shoulders. Nobody could go in or out while their watch was maintained. Then, using an unmarked dark-blue mid-sized Chevy, he and a woman constable ventured slowly along the trail. At first there were dwellings and farm installations, then the roadway narrowed and trees arched overhead. About a mile and three-quarters along the track, the constable, who was at the wheel, suddenly slowed and peered out of the window to her left, where stretches of recent weed growth towered and ran wild. 'Hey,' she said.

'What is it, Marcia?'

'I think we ought to take a look around,' she answered. 'I recognize this property, Ralph. This was supposed to be the Coronet Realty Development. A dozen four-bedroom units for upscale buyers.'

'What happened to it?'

'The land turned out to be mostly hardrock shelving and they couldn't dig foundations or lay pipe. It's waste land. I guess those weeds can grow on anything. Look at them! Some of them must be ten feet tall.'

The two officers got out of the car as quietly as possible, then tiptoed along an almost invisible path through the weeds until they found themselves on a flat shelf of ancient limestone. At a distance of maybe 300 feet (or about one hundred metres, Ralph thought) stood a huge old barn, the work perhaps of the original settlers who had long ago discovered that this land could not be farmed.

'How could they build a thing that size, when they can't put in four-bedroom houses?' Ralph asked Marcia. She answered him scornfully, 'Don't need a foundation for a barn. You ever see a barn with a rec room?' Marcia was a country girl.

'Come on,' she whispered, 'let's go around in back.' They worked their way around to the left and soon found themselves in swamp which kept them from circling right around the building. But in behind it, just visible from where they were standing, was a helicopter tethered to heavy pegs and protected from the weather by great sheets of clear plastic.

'That clinches it,' Ralph said. He saw that the case was breaking fast. He and Marcia hurried back to the car, where they established radio contact with OPP Gananoque, requesting a check with the county records office in Stoverville on ownership of this land, formerly the site of a projected housing development financed by Coronet Realty. Withing half an hour the answer was flashed to them. Coronet Realty was part of a pyramid of financial structures underpinned by Millsaps Investments.

'Over and out,' said Marcia. She relayed this information to Corporal Cavan, who now ordered her to open communication with the two patrol cars stationed at either end of the road. Each car carried four men, equipped with full riot-control and assault equipment. They weren't exactly a SWAT team. Their vehicles weren't armoured and they didn't have flame-throwers or much in the way of tear gas. But they weren't likely to face major defensive firepower anyway. By early afternoon eight heavily armed constables were prowling and prowling around the barn like the hosts of Midian, often getting stuck in the gumbo deposits which lay in the deep seams of the rock face. The operation was conducted more or less silently, surprise being preserved almost to the end, on both sides of the confrontation. It might have been Corporal Cavan's failure to deploy his force so as to surround the objective which allowed the escape. Cavan argued at the inquiry that he hadn't had enough men at his disposal to cover the whole area.

At about 14:00 hours a male figure made his way out of a rear exit of the barn in the direction of the tethered 'copter. That the escapee was male was established by forensic examination of boot tracks and on the basis of visual observation made in the following stage of the operation. At 14:10 the escapee must have succeeded in letting go the helicopter's moorings. A minute or two later the craft's rotor was activated with a sudden clattering sound. Corporal Cavan's men stood still in their tracks, uncertain whether or not to fire at the getaway attempt. After all, they maintained at the inquiry, it was mainly a matter of some birds. They couldn't bring down a helicopter, and risk injuring somebody who might be proved innocent of any major crime. They weren't in radio communication with the operational commander at that specific moment. The corporal later maintained that he had given loud verbal instructions to fire at the rotors, but in fact nobody used his or her weapon. The helicopter rose rapidly out of range and in a few minutes was merely a speck in the distance.

'Request intervention CFB Trenton,' shrieked Cavan into his transmitter, but he got no effective results. OPP weren't about to ask Trenton to scramble jet fighters to intercept an unidentified helicopter. There just wasn't that much at stake. So the craft made its way to some secret escape point and its occupant or occupants – there may have been as many as three – were never afterwards captured.

Rumours persist of a Millsaps sighting in Panama City, but without a positive identification Canadian diplomacy is powerless to make representations towards extradition.

At barn-site Corporal Cavan was in a state of controlled hysteria as he saw his chief suspect disappear into the blue. Angered and vengeful, he gave orders to storm the barn and effect entry. He was now certain that there was nobody inside and he felt a bitter satisfaction as he watched his men breaking open the wide sliding doors at either end of the building. All at once the chains and locks gave way, the doors rolled silently back on oiled runners. With a great sound the birds emerged and escaped into the upper air. They had been uncaged in the barn, allowed to run tame and free in their hundreds.

One Christmas as a very young child Ralph Cavan had found a little kaleidoscope in his stocking. Without knowing what it was or what it did, he put the eyepiece to his eye and squinted down the narrow dark tube towards the mysterious coloured pattern at the other end. Snowflakes, he thought, coloured snowflakes, purple, green, red, yellow. He put his small hand on the other end of the instrument and accidentally found out how to work it. He twisted the barrel of the toy and the pattern he had been eyeing fell apart and reconstructed itself in an entirely different order. He gave a squeak of sheer innocent pleasure and twisted the thing again, and again the magical colours linked and separated and exfoliated and were reborn in new forms. He turned and turned his toy and the brilliant flakes of colour danced and spun and tumbled apart and glowed and piled themselves up.

Now as he stood on a squelchy tuft of grassy mud sunk in an old limestone seam, he looked up at the glittering sky and saw the same colour-event, flaming and shining bits of brightness forming and parting and falling this way and that and rising again acrobatically, circling and parading across his field of vision. Christmas. It will be Christmas in six weeks and the nights will grow very cold.

You'll Catch Your Death

YOU GO DOWN TWO FLIGHTS of concrete steps and through a pair of heavy metal doors back where the washrooms are. Then you come into Place Versailles, the boutique complex beside the bargain basement. The first thing you see is a shop specializing in women's footwear that calls itself BOOT EEK!

The store beside it sells nightwear and lingerie and goes by the name TANTE ALICE!

None of the shops is closed in, and they don't meet at right angles. You walk in and out and through them, with the music from the record shop very loud, the colours of all the little booths clashing and contrasting, purple, orange, lime-green. Earth-shaking announcements levelled at bargain hunters. Little sit-down counters selling pizza slices or bagels. Strange orange mushroom-shaped benches. Chilling breezes from the air-conditioning, crowds swirling at your back while you sit and chew, and then the birdcalls and the yapping and mewing from BGS, where Sandy and her crowd hang out.

Do you know what it's like? It's like a never-ending world's fair or trade show. Walls plastered with murals in party colours: wooden soldiers in red coats with fluffball buttons parading down their chests. Cutouts of the front ends of gondolas, shiny black profiles of the Eiffel Tower, display dummies holding out their arms to you. Birds' voices, are they frightened? Do they like it here?

BGS is the most popular hangout at this level, close to the downtown campus and the Cinéplex entryway; you can reach the Métro station without going outside. You can get anything you want to eat nearby. There's a McDonald's at the other end of the building, free newspapers and warmth. Everybody comes to BGS sooner or later. Sandy's boyfriend Stoner is an assistant manager there while he goes to school. He's quit and been fired and re-hired and gone on nights and put in unlimited overtime and paid his way through an

African Studies program, but now, almost in sight of his BA, he's switching to the theatre program; he believes he can make it as an actor. So he'll be an assistant manager at BGs for a while yet. Sandy doesn't mind; she loves the atmosphere of the pet shop and besides, that's where she met Stoner. He sold her our first bird ten years ago. It was birthday money; it's how we got started with our birds. There's a brotherhood and sisterhood of bird-lovers and collectors, a closed society. There may even be an élitist angle to this. People who know about birds don't relate well to the rest of the world.

Sandy brought home our first bird when she was sixteen. She called him or her – we're not sure – Candy, because he was so sweet and it rhymed with Sandy. He learned his name right away but he never learned hers and he seemed more ready to bond with me than her. I didn't ask for it; I'm only her mother, but I finger-trained Candy and I've always cleaned the cages. Ronnie and Bingo arrived later. We've only got the three medium-sized birds, Candy Cockatiel, Ronnie Reagan the lorikeet, and our youngest, Bingo, the little purple-masked conure. We keep them in different rooms, otherwise nobody could hold a conversation, except with them of course. We haven't encouraged them to talk. It's enough to hear Candy, Candy, Candy, Candy, Candy, Candy, Candy. But what are you going to do? You have to take some responsibility.

Sandy has taught Ronnie Reagan to meow, a dumb thing to do if you ask me. He only meows for her and you really can't tell it from a cat. Luckily she's not around the house much in the daytime. She'll be down at the main campus or else at BGs with the gang. Stoner, Hèléne, Marie-Josée. Carla graduated at the end of the last semester and moved to Bahrein. And the bag ladies, two or three of them that come over from McDonald's around ten a.m. A couple of them are in their eighties, I think, with those grey herringbone overcoats belted in the back, trailing on the muddy parquet. They have their bags, and they sit outside the pet shop eating whatever it is they eat. I don't know that they could show ten good teeth between them. Nobody understands what they say, and they don't actually come into the shop.

Then there's Maggie. She might be twenty years younger than

the other ladies. She used to meet them every morning at McDonald's around nine, to read the morning papers and have something to eat. I don't know that she ever did much cooking or housekeeping where she lived. She really only had the one room and a little kitchen alcove. It might have been cheaper just to have something at McDonald's every day. But she wasn't one of the homeless people. I think the two older ones just spent the night wherever they happened to be when the malls closed, but Maggie had a home to go to.

She was allowed into BGs. She was one of the bird people. I think she had more feeling for them than anybody I know. As soon as she and the two bag ladies arrived in the morning she'd settle the old ones on the bench outside. Maybe an hour or two later they'd drift off somewhere, mumbling to themselves and poking in the refuse torpedoes. Sandy once told me that one of them found a purse in a refuse bin with over fifty dollars in it. She didn't seem to know what the money was, just turned the stuff over to a security guard. I'll bet you that fifty bucks never found its way home. Those really old ones are right out of it, you know that?

Maggie had an interest in life to keep her going. She never got in anybody's way but every morning around eleven-thirty you'd see her creeping into the pet shop space. You couldn't really keep her out because there wasn't any door, just the sliding glass panel that got padlocked shut after closing. She didn't smell like the others; you could smell them coming a block away, body odour, stale food, and some sort of funny sweetish smell. Nobody wanted them inside a boutique but Maggie was different. She wasn't pushy, she didn't smell. She came every day just before lunch. Once or twice Stoner asked her to keep an eye on the store while he went to the washroom. I suppose he shouldn't have done that because he was responsible for the stock, the birds and animals, the cages, the selection of pet-lovers' books, bird books, cat books. The boxes of ant-eggs and bags of sunflower seeds and the displays of rubber bones and cat toys. A big inventory. But there wasn't much of a problem with theft at the pet shop. I mean, who steals cat toys? Except other cats of course. I'm no cat lover. Cats attack birds.

Mr Slonim just happened to come by while poor Stoner was gone for a pee, leaving Maggie alone in the shop. That was one of the times Stoner got fired; the boss didn't like finding Maggie in charge, actually trying to handle a sale. She had most of her teeth but she never spoke too clearly and it's always very noisy out at the front of the store.

'You're fired again, Stoner, this time it's definitive. Go on, beat it, and take that old bag with you.'

'OK, Mr Slonim. You know where to find me if you need me.'

The boss always hires Stoner back after a while. He knows the stock and something about pet care, and he's a willing boy, I'll certainly say that for him. I like old Stoner. He was very kind to Maggie. He kind of adopted her, he and Sandy. I used to hear about her from them; they always called her 'the bird lady'.

'The bird lady was around again all day. You know, Mom, I almost believe she really talks to them. Or she thinks she does. I guess it's the same thing, really.' Sandy is too tender-hearted for her own good.

'I don't know if she eats enough.'

'Who?'

'Maggie, the bird lady. She can't have very much money.'

'Wouldn't she have some kind of pension or welfare or that?'

'You know, Mom, I don't think anybody can really live, not to say really *live*, on welfare.'

'Don't think about it. It's none of your business. If the bird lady gets into trouble, she'll let you know.'

'I guess so. You ought to see her feeding the birds. It's obvious, Mom, she loves them. Do you think we could have her out to dinner sometime? Would that be a good thing to do? I'd help you serve and do the cleaning up. There's only going to be four of us, you and me and Daddy and Maggie.'

'Or we might pick some night when your Dad has to work. Ask her for a Tuesday or a Thursday, Sandy, and find out what she likes to eat.'

'Oh, she probably eats like a bird.'

'Birds spend their lifetime looking for food,' I said.

'Oh, Mom, don't be so *realistic*.'

A week or two later we had her out to the house for the evening. She was just bowled over by our pets; she stood in front of Candy's cage for three-quarters of an hour repeating, 'Say your name, Birdie, say your name,' and 'Who's a good bird, then?' But the one she was really ready to fall in love with was Ronnie Reagan, who vocalizes all the time. 'Is he our little Mister President? Such a good little Mister President. Say hello, Ronnie, hello Ronnie. Doesn't he have his own little Nancy? Maggie will be his Nancy, that's right. Say Nancy!'

The bird actually whistled something that sounded like Nancy, and I thought Maggie was going to flip. We had to drag her away from the birds and almost force her to eat. I'd have thought she'd be hungry; she didn't look properly nourished. She told us that she'd been trying to save enough money to buy a bird of her own but she just didn't seem to be able to manage it. When she said this, Sandy grinned at me across the table and shook her head unobtrusively. I didn't understand what she meant just then, but I found out later that the gang at BGs were on the lookout for an unsaleable bird that they could buy on discount and give to Maggie.

'I just envy you and Sandy so much. Say hello, Ronnie, that's right.'

'Will you have some more lamb? Another potato?'

'Oh, no, I couldn't eat another bite, thank you.'

She'd left a bit of potato and a bit of meat and a few peas at the side of her plate.

'Can you manage dessert?'

'Perhaps just a small piece.' We were having lemon pie, and it made a hit with her. 'This was my very favourite when I was a girl, lemon meringue pie. Doesn't it taste good?'

'I made the crust myself,' I said, 'but the filling is from a mix.'

'If you hadn't told me I'd never have guessed,' she said. 'I wonder, could I have just a tiny bit more?' She ate three pieces. She certainly was dying for something sweet.

After she went home Sandy told me that she and Stoner and Marie-Josée and Hèléne, and even Mr Slonim, had agreed to pass the hat and contribute the purchase price on the first small bird that came into the store with a deformity or a handicap. Birds are expensive; you can pay almost any amount for a desirable item, an African Grey or a cockatoo or a macaw. Even smaller ones can run to several hundred dollars, and then there are the start-up costs, cage equipment and food and books on training and diet and little objects to keep your bird amused, mirrors, cuttlebones, swings and bells. It all adds up. A starter kit for tropical bird care might run you anything up to five hundred dollars not counting the price of the bird itself or continuing expenses like food, vitamins and other dietary supplements, and periodic visits to the vet.

So the plan was to keep an eye out for a damaged specimen and some low-cost equipment, a used cage and a supply of food at post-holiday sale prices. Then they'd present Maggie with everything at once including her very own bird, on her birthday if possible. The one snag was that nobody could get her to reveal her age or her birth date. I'm not even sure that anybody around the pet shop knew her full name.

Eventually a damaged specimen turned up, a pretty little parakeet with shiny green plumage and yellow flares under each wing, just a darling little bird but unfortunately born with a malformed left claw that made it hard for him to grip a perch properly. Otherwise he was in perfect condition and might live a long time, providing companionship for Maggie as she got older. I think she was already much older than anybody imagined. She had one of those faces with very smooth grey skin, criss-crossed by a network of almost invisible wrinkles. You didn't notice the lines until you got up close to her and then the effect was surprising, almost – I hate to say this – almost repulsive. She gave the impression of somebody aging twenty years from one moment to the next.

Mr Slonim charged the gang $100 for the parakeet, less employee discount, and then he knocked off fifteen bucks from the price as his contribution. He let Stoner make up a starter kit including cage, water and food dishes, a cuttlebone, a swing, two perches, and a supply of food, for another $50. Then they all got together one afternoon in May and shepherded Maggie out of the store for an hour – I think they took her for pizza – while Sandy made up a presentation display. They put the parakeet into his new cage and selected perches that wouldn't be too much of a trial for his poor little claw. He seemed right at home, and went straight to his water dish. Then he climbed around on the bars for a while and then everybody came back with Maggie and they held a presentation.

'We claim it's your birthday, Maggie. We've decided you must be a Taurus but you won't admit anything, so we've picked out today. Stoner has something he wants to tell you.'

She just stood there and gaped at them; she couldn't seem to believe what was happening.

'Maggie,' said Stoner, 'we've decided that you're a world-class bird fancier, and we think you ought to have a bird of your own to take care of you. So seeing as it's your birthday....'

'It's not my birthday. I never claimed it was my birthday.'

'It's your *official* birthday, just like the Queen has. So a few of us got together and picked out this little parakeet as a present for you. And here he is!'

He picked up the cage from a nearby stand and showed it to Maggie. He thought she was going to have a stroke on the spot. She couldn't make much sense. She just kept mumbling, 'For me?'

'What are you going to call him, Maggie?'

Everybody was curious to know what name she'd choose.

There was quite a long pause, totally silent except for the noise from the record store and the loudspeakers and the crowd filing past. Mr Slonim started to fidget.

'I'm going to call him Bentley,' she said at last.

Nobody ever figured that one out. Bentley? There was a lot of laughter and clapping. Then Mr Slonim started to issue commands.

'Break-time's over, everybody; let's see a little action here. Let's dispose of some puppies and kittens today. OK, Stoner. The party's over. We're open till nine p.m. in this location, everybody, just come on in and browse around!'

So there was Maggie, sitting on a bench a few feet away from the pet shop, with the cage and its cover, and a pile of equipment in bags and boxes, with Bentley hopping around in his cage, making a loud noise for such a little guy. It took her an hour to pull herself together; she'd been flabbergasted by the presentation, and kept repeating that it wasn't really her birthday, it just felt like it. Around four-thirty Sandy and one of her girlfriends helped the poor old thing home that night, 'in one room with a sink and a mini-fridge, and a toilet and shower down the hall. I didn't think that anybody lived like that now.'

'Plenty of people live like that,' I said, 'that is, if they've got any place to go at all.'

'Stoner has been cast in *The Importance of Being Earnest*,' she said. 'He thinks it's a breakthrough for him.'

'He's got a good heart, Sandy,' I said, 'but he'll never take Broadway by storm.'

Excitement over Stoner's progress in the theatre programme seemed to preoccupy Sandy and her friends at the pet shop for most of the summer. Casting had been announced in early June; the play was to be the first offering in the fall dramatic season at the theatre school. We didn't hear any more about Maggie through the summer and early fall, except that Bentley was doing well and enjoying his new quarters. Maggie didn't come into the shop nearly as often as before; she felt that she had to be near Bentley. Stoner had supplied her with a couple of stick perches for preliminary training; when she came in to buy sunflower seeds she used to report on his progress.

'He hops onto the stick all right, but he has trouble balancing.

'I've shaved his stick perches down and now he just loves them.

'He's out of the cage now, and sits on my wrist.

'We're well into finger-training.

'I've got him to walk up my arm to the elbow.

'He knows his name and he talks to me all the time.

'Now he knows *my* name!

'He sits on my shoulder and walks around behind my neck.

'Bentley's been to the vet for his six-months checkup. She says he's in perfect health.

'He perches on the doorframe.

'He sings like an angel.'

If you ask me, Maggie took better care of that bird than she did of herself. She was in the shop one afternoon in mid-November, and according to Stoner she looked like she was coming down with something serious: poor colour and a rasp in her throat.

Stoner said, 'After that I kept an eye on her, and she didn't look to me like she was throwing it off. She'd come in and pick up food items for Bentley, and she'd tell us how he was getting along, but actually we were seeing less and less of her. Then this last time she came in looking like the wrath of God, grey and tired and trembling. I told her – I practically ordered her – to go home and get into a hot bath and go to bed.'

'She hasn't got a tub, Stoner, only a shower,' Sandy said.

'Well, whatever,' he said. 'Go on home and get under the covers. You'll catch your death hanging around here. Go on, Maggie, beat it! We bird fanciers know what's best for each other.'

She took his advice and disappeared into the crowd of holiday shoppers, and nobody heard anything more about her for a while. Christmas came and went, the most disagreeable Christmas on record because of the power failures. New Year's was wet and sloppy and messy. Sandy grumped around the house; she and Stoner were having some sort of temporary falling-out. January in Montréal is no picnic.

Then I got this phone call last Monday, nobody I recognized, a quiet, deep male voice, asking if anybody at our number knew Margaret Fitzwilliams.

'I don't think so,' I said, 'there's nobody here by that name.'

'No, madame,' he said, 'I was asking if you knew her.'

'I certainly do not. May I ask how you got this number?'

'It's written down here on a scrap of paper, beside the name Sandy. Do you have a Sandy there?'

'That's our daughter, but she doesn't know any Margaret Fitzwilliams.'

Suddenly his voice got brisk and alert. 'I hear birds on the phone, madame. Do you happen to have birds in your home?'

'Why, yes, we do. May I ask who's calling?'

'I'm a police officer, madame, investigating an unexplained death. You see, there's a dead bird in the room, as well as the dead lady.'

'My God,' I said, 'I think you must be talking about Maggie, the bird lady. That's who it is. Is she elderly, living in one room, grey hair, thin, probably alone?'

'That describes her correctly.'

'Well, that's a friend of my daughter's from BGs pet shop in Place Versailles. I never knew her last name; everybody just called her Maggie the bird lady. What should I tell my daughter?'

'Would you ask her please to get in touch with me, Sergeant Ladouceur?' He gave his office phone number. 'We need a positive identification and information about her family and associates. There's the question of burial, you see, and certain other technicalities. We can't do anything here; the power's been off for two days. We're going to remove the body but there's a bit of cleaning up to do, so if you'll ask your daughter to phone in....'

Sandy came in late from the first meeting of one of her winter semester courses. I put off saying anything till she'd had a chance to eat something hot. Then I told her the news and gave her the policeman's local. She was terribly upset and insisted on getting in touch with him right away. Those policemen must work around the clock.

Next morning she and Stoner went downtown to make the identification. It was Maggie all right. Cause of death was pneumonia with complications and congestive heart failure, with a general condition of near starvation. The landlord had gone into her room and found her during the power failure, when nobody had seen her for days.

The way the police explained the death, she'd gone to bed to keep warm during the power failure. After it had been going on for a long time Bentley died of the cold, and when she realized that she just stopped caring for herself. There was untouched food in her little fridge and quite a supply of sunflower seeds on the table. She probably felt very weak from chest congestion and from not eating and finally her heart gave out.

After they made the identification, Stoner and Sandy went back to BGS to let some of the gang know what had happened. Stoner booked off work; he didn't feel like working that evening. He and Sandy and Marie-Josée and Mr Slonim went for pizza around seven p.m., and sat together on one of those orange plastic mushrooms outside the store, chewing away at the tacky pizza slices and drinking their coffee quickly before it could get cold. It struck them that energy and power failures were becoming general. They could no longer expect to live better electrically.

Other Books by Hugh Hood

NOVELS

White Figure, White Ground 1964
The Camera Always Lies 1967
A Game of Touch 1970
You Cant Get There from Here 1972
Five New Facts About Giorgione 1987

The New Age/Le nouveau siècle:

I: *The Swing in the Garden* 1975
II: *A New Athens* 1977
III: *Reservoir Ravine* 1979
IV: *Black and White Keys* 1982
V: *The Scenic Art* 1984
VI: *The Motor Boys in Ottawa* 1986
VII: *Tony's Book* 1988
VIII: *Property and Value* 1990

STORIES

Flying a Red Kite 1962
Around the Mountain: Scenes from Montréal Life 1967
The Fruit Man, the Meat Man and the Manager 1971
Dark Glasses 1976
Selected Stories 1978
None Genuine Without This Signature 1980
August Nights 1985
A Short Walk in the Rain 1989
The Isolation Booth 1991

NON-FICTION